DIVORCING JACK

DIVORCING JACK

A screenplay by
COLIN BATEMAN

Based on the novel by Colin Bateman

HarperCollins*Publishers*

For Andrea and Matthew

HarperCollins*Publishers*
77–85 Fulham Palace Road,
Hammersmith, London W6 8JB

A Paperback Original 1998
1 3 5 7 9 8 6 4 2

Copyright © Colin Bateman 1998

The Author asserts the moral right to
be identified as the author of this work

A catalogue record for this book
is available from the British Library

ISBN 0 00 651274 7

Film stills and photographs by Marcus Robinson

Set in Plantin Light

Printed and bound in Great Britain by
Caledonian International Book Manufacturing Ltd, Glasgow

INTRODUCTION

I think you can define people's true musical taste by what they listen to when they're drunk, not what's fashionable or new, but what scratched twelve inches of plastic they manage to get on to the record player in the early hours of the morning and blast, even though they can barely stand. With me it's punk, and not just punk, but The Clash. Many's the time I've had the police at the door asking me to turn Joe Strummer down.

I loved The Clash. Still do. Naturally, when I wrote *Divorcing Jack,* the novel, it not only featured their music but the whole spirit of The Clash imbued the story. Or so I like to think. I don't know The Clash personally; I worship from afar. No – not worship – admire, not just great rock'n'roll, but attitude and the ability to change and grow up. The Clash. More Of This Later.

I never really wanted to be in a band. Possibly because I knew I was without any musical ability. Even the three chords of punk were three too many. (I did at one point buy a synthesiser, when they were just getting popular in the very early eighties, figuring you didn't have to tune it, but needless to say I couldn't make head nor tail of it and I ended up selling it to A Christian.) I compensated by managing a few bands (badly), and even releasing a couple of records for them; the unsold copies still prop up my bed. I opened a rock club in my home town of Bangor. If you don't know Bangor, it's a nice quiet dormitory town a dozen miles from Belfast. Our mean streets are actually cul-de-sacs. Three people turned up on the first night of my rock club and I still demanded my ten per cent of the door from the band and they told me to Fuck Off. I said okay. And I did.

No, my dream was to be a writer. Always was. When I was eight or nine I remember demanding a typewriter for Christmas. And then being so disappointed when Santa brought one of those crap Chad Valley efforts that printed big blue smudgy letters. How was I supposed to write the Great American Novel on that? (Who would want to write the Great Northern Ireland Novel? And Ireland was a foreign country back then.) The opening scene of this screenplay features my brother pissing into that typewriter case. Some people might find this disgusting. I think it's quite admirable to be able even to find a receptacle capable of holding that amount of pish while in such a state of inebriation.

Getting a job on the local paper was the first step to a writing career. I spent ten years writing a column which started with punk rock and over time evolved into something else. Taking the piss (but not the pish) and talking nonsense, mostly.

But I was always determined to write a novel, although I had no idea what about. I tried my hand at poems and short stories – the easy options. (I don't wish to demean either, but at least you can produce a finished poem in an hour; you can hold it up and say, look, I've written a poem. You can finish a short story in a night. If you can write a novel in one night, you're a genius or fucking bonkers. It's a long haul. You have to switch off *Coronation Street* for months and forget Liverpool for an entire season.)

But look what it gets you: The Clash. More Of This Later.

Divorcing Jack was written for fun, just to see if I could do it, but it came about after many years of staring at other people's excellent books and getting depressed because I knew I could never write like that.

And then one day it dawned on me (like puberty, although not so much fun), that I couldn't write those other books, because they'd already been written. If I was going to write at all it would have to be my words, my thoughts, from inside of me, right deep down to my Union Jack socks. And so I set to work with the merest sliver of an idea which came to me in the bath, a play on words featuring the phrase 'Divorcing Jack'.

Don't ask me where it came from.

I mean, with *Moby Dick*, you can probably guess how it came to yer man in the bath. But Divorcing Jack? I don't know.

Just thank God. All I wanted to write was a good, fun book, an adventure, a good laugh, *The Thirty-Nine Steps* with a complete eejit on the run rather than a dashing hero. In retrospect I was, of course, trying to write a blackly comic satire on the Troubles, even if at the time I was just trying to get to the end of each chapter.

Divorcing Jack was written over the course of a year, finished, posted, returned, posted, returned, posted, returned, posted, returned, about thirty times over the course of another year. Nobody liked it. I gave up on it. Stuck it in a drawer. My girlfriend, now my wife, was on at me to let her read it, but if agents and publishers thought it was crap, a mere mortal wasn't going to have the opportunity to tell me I was useless as well.

But eventually, as they do, she got to me, and read it and really, genuinely loved it. She persuaded me to send it to HarperCollins, one of the biggest publishers in the world, and within a couple of weeks they were in touch to say they loved it and suddenly I was an Author and People Took Me Seriously.

I had always thought authors had an insight into the meaning of life and the way of the world. That they understood

Shakespeare and poetry and philosophy and knew exactly what quote from the classics to start their novels with.

Whereas I knew only the correct wrist action needed to remove the stiff lid on a jar of Hartley's Raspberry Jam.

Then, one day, the BBC called.

The BBC!

They wanted to make a film!

My wife, in her wisdom, having been right once, after all, and responsible for All Of This, made me wear a suit to that first meeting. I suppose they were laughing into their sleeves because I looked like I was going for my confirmation.

Expensive restaurant. Loved the book. They had somebody lined up to do the screenplay already. I didn't mind, at first, because they made TV shows and movies all the time while I was only starting out. The book hadn't even been published yet.

But if you think publishing is slow, you should try movies. A couple of years passed. I'd published three moderately successful novels. The BBC, admirably, hung in there trying to raise the cash while I gained confidence in my writing and no longer wore a suit when I had to meet them. Then the BBC hooked up with Scala, the company that had risen from the ashes of the cool and trendy Palace Pictures and which had chalked up a big hit with *The Crying Game* and suddenly all systems were go. Except this time I was asked to write the screenplay.

This is it.

The director was to be David Caffrey, a young Dubliner making a name for himself with his short films. The star was to be Robert Carlyle, best known as TV cop Hamish Macbeth, who'd just finished making some trifle called *The Full Monty*.

I set to work.

People now ask me all the time how I write screenplays and

what the difficulties are in adapting your own novel and I tell them that I have no idea.

I just do it. Sit down and type.

There is a certain structure to a movie, but I'll be buggered if I can tell you what it is. If you've watched a lot of movies, you'll know. You may not be able to tell someone or write it down, but you'll know. You know that there are certain types of shots. That you need to keep things zipping along. That you can't have pages and pages of static dialogue (even Woody Allen doesn't, despite what you might think). That some things you write cannot be said by actors and will have to be changed. That it must build towards a climax. All that stuff.

Screenwriting is also a team game, and if you're lucky that team is one you want to play for. You can write a reasonably good first draft in two or three weeks, but from there on in it's a question of going through it line by line, scene by scene, with the director and/or producer, to knock it into a shape that hopefully combines your vision with that of the director's, while the producer contributes his vast experience and keeps his eye on the practicalities. You don't always all agree, and the writer, traditionally, is the guy who gets shat upon most regularly, but there is a simple choice you have to make: stay on the team bus, and have the chance of playing, or get off and walk home in the rain with your hands in your pockets. It isn't your ball any more, you've sold it to the big guy with the shades. If you stay and play you have a chance of influencing the game and you might occasionally be able to pop up and score. Enough of the football analogies (although I was and still am a greedy bastard on the ball).

Divorcing Jack had, I think, a good team. It was David Caffrey's big break into movies and he was a bundle of nervous energy throughout, constantly thinking of new ideas and egging me on to come up with something better. Producer

Robert Cooper, whose day job is head of drama at BBC Northern Ireland, was the Figure of Authority but his ideas were absolutely spot on and he made sure the script stayed as close to the tone of the book as possible instead of veering off into some of the implausible wackiness we came up with in the pub on a Saturday afternoon. Robert Carlyle pulled out and was replaced by David Thewlis, star of *Naked*, a film I didn't particularly like, but his performance in it was mind-blowing. A good guy, and he got the accent spot on. Previously, I'd been asked what film star I'd like to play Dan Starkey and had never been able to make my mind up. But the moment I met David Thewlis, he was the one.

Divorcing Jack and my other movie, *Cycle of Violence*, now retitled *Crossmaheart*, were the first films for many years to be made entirely on location in Northern Ireland and it was a privilege and a pleasure to work on them. I always felt it was important that they were made there, instead of in Manchester or Dublin where all the other scaredy-cat Northern Ireland films are made, and I think everyone involved was constantly surprised by the level of co-operation and support they received throughout the shooting. Of course, we had to get special permission to do actual shooting with guns 'n' stuff. People from outside tend to think of the Province as some vast war zone, but it's actually quite peaceful and very small. (Case in point: when *Divorcing Jack* was filming I was surprised to find that the paperback went back into the local charts, just for one week. Then I realised that the film company had advertised for extras, and they'd all gone out and bought a copy to read up. That's how small it is.)

This screenplay is basically the shooting script, but lines get changed, scenes cut, voice overs added, and as I write this I haven't seen the finished movie, so God knows what they've done to my words. If it's excellent, I'm quite happy to take all the credit. If it's crap, that director . . .

However, the whole point of this is that a few months ago I was sitting in the production office with the manager of The Clash.

Joe Strummer from the band had written a song called 'Divorcing Jack'.

How your life comes full circle and dreams come true.

But it wasn't selected for the movie. They chose, instead, The Nolan Sisters.

The Nolans.

The Nolans or Joe Strummer. We'll have The Nolans.

Which meant that there was a song out there by Joe Strummer called 'Divorcing Jack' which was never going to see the light of day. I mean, what else could he use it for?

I had to have it. So this thirty-five-year-old man writes a fan/begging letter to Joe Strummer, and a couple of weeks later a tape of the song and a nice letter arrive on my doormat.

My own personal Clash song.

See? Life comes full circle and dreams do come true. That's Hollywood. Or Pinewood.

So switch off *Coronation Street* and write your own novel or screenplay. You might end up with your own personal Clash song.

Or at least one by the Nolans.

Colin Bateman
March 1998

INT. BEDROOM – NIGHT

We see a child's bedroom at night. Eight-year-old Dan Starkey is asleep. The bedroom door opens and a figure enters, but it is too dark to see clearly. The figure stumbles and bangs off furniture.

Dan begins to stir. There is silence, then the sound of a zip going down and, oddly, of a stream of water against plastic, followed by a sigh of relief.

> STARKEY
> *(v/o)*

When I was eight I woke up in the middle of the night and found my brother pissing in my typewriter case.

Dan switches on the bedside light.

> DAN

Davie. What're you –

His brother turns, pissed and pissing, spraying urine around him. Dan dives back under the covers, laughing, while his brother stumbles around the room, soaking it with urine, then crashes over toys and books to collapse on the other bed, already snoring.

> STARKEY
> *(v/o)*

I decided there and then there was something wonderful about alcohol. As my artistic interest grew, I discovered that many of my heroes had had impassioned affairs with what my old da referred to as 'the devil's vomit'.

There are pictures on the wall, framed photos, concert posters.

STARKEY
(v/o)
Brendan Behan, Dylan Thomas, George Best, Pete Townshend. It had not adversely affected any of them.
(Beat)
With the exception of the first two, whom it killed.

TITLES OVER:

INT. STARKEY'S HOUSE – BEDROOM

An alarm goes off. The bed clothes are thrown back to show the adult Starkey. He's young, sharp-eyed and cheeky faced. He ignores the alarm as he pads across to the bathroom, picking up a can of beer from the floor as he goes.

There is a woman in the bed behind him, just beginning to wake. Her hand reaches out, turns off the alarm, then flops back down. This is his wife, Patricia.

In the bathroom, Starkey pours the beer down the sink, then opens a bottle of headache pills, pours two out, then two more, and swallows them.

EXT. BUS – DAY

Starkey is on a bus on his way to work, his head against the window. He is almost asleep again, head jerking, eyes flickering.

We see Belfast street scenes, but not the war-like images familiar from the news. Paramilitary murals are being whitewashed;

2

lampposts and walls are plastered with election posters; the word BRINN *stands out, although there are other names in different colours.*

EXT. STREET – DAY

As Starkey steps on to the pavement from the bus, he is offered an election flyer. He takes it and the name BRINN *is just visible before he crumples it up and drop-kicks it. As he walks away from the bus we see that the side of the vehicle is entirely taken up with a smiling portrait of Brinn.*

INT. NEWSPAPER OFFICE – DAY

A newspaper office coming up to press time: a scene of frantic activity, for everyone except Dan Starkey, who is staring listlessly at his screen.

Taped to his work station is a large photograph of an

imposing-looking man, recognisable as Michael Brinn, except the eyes have been cut out, making him look demonic.

WOODS

Starkey!

Starkey jolts round to see his editor, Frankie Woods, middle-aged, overweight, hassled, standing in the doorway of his office across the newsroom. Woods raises one finger and curls it back, summoning him.

A reporter at the desk opposite Starkey, looking even more hassled, puts his phone down and calls to him:

MOUSE

Dan! You still okay about that?

STARKEY

What?

MOUSE

That thing, y'know. Y'okay?

STARKEY

Mouse, look . . . what?

MOUSE

Dan. The PR thing. The American.

STARKEY

Yuh . . . Yeah, sorry, I'm . . . *New York Times*, right?

MOUSE

Boston Globe. Dan, c'mon, you will turn up?

4

STARKEY

Of course I will . . .

INT. EDITOR'S OFFICE – DAY

Frankie Woods is pacing the office, reading aloud from Starkey's copy. Dan stands before his desk. As they talk a succession of people enter, putting down photos, computer disks, page lay-outs. We catch glimpses of potential headlines: ADAMS DECOMMISSIONS ARMS, PAISLEY DECOMMISSIONS ADAMS . . .

WOODS

Just in off the wires: 'If elected, Michael Brinn is going to swap Belfast for the Guinness Brewery in Dublin; they can have our troubles and we can drink theirs . . .'. Bollocks!

STARKEY

I'm only trying to –

WOODS
(Still reading)
'Michael Brinn's going to sponsor paramilitary coffee mornings, with an Armalite in one hand and a packet of Jaffa Cakes in the other . . .' It's shite!

STARKEY

You pay me to write shite like that.

WOODS

I pay you to write shite that's funny.

5

STARKEY

It's satire!

WOODS

My point exactly! For godsake, man, we're going
independent here, we're talking happy, optimistic, joyous.
We've thrown our weight behind Michael Brinn, Dan,
you know what our line is.

STARKEY

Aye. He's the one man who can knit it all together, bring
a lasting peace . . .
(Beat)
Are you going to print it or what?

Woods stares at him, then walks to his desk with the copy.

WOODS

Only because we've a fuckin' hole to fill. But do me a
favour, Dan, lay off him for a while. Do what you do
best: get out there, get me a story, get your ear to the
ground, okay?

EXT. PARK – DAY

*Starkey's ear, and the rest of his head, hit a gravelled path in a
public park. We pull back to see a beautiful young woman,
Margaret, looking concerned. On the seat behind Starkey is a
plastic-topped crate of lager, with a hole in the plastic where he's
been removing cans.*

MARGARET

Are you okay?

Starkey blinks back into semi-consciousness.

6

STARKEY

Can you keep out of the light? I'm working.

MARGARET

Uh-huh.

STARKEY

Gravel Inspector. Department of Stones.

He sits up and brushes the gravel from his face and coat. Margaret shakes her head.

MARGARET

I thought you'd cracked your head.

STARKEY

I did crack my head.
                    (He rubs his head)
I think it's broken.

She smiles and then retreats to the next bench along, where her bag is sitting with a bottle of wine sticking out of it. While Starkey picks himself up, she pointedly looks away and glances at her watch; she's obviously waiting for someone.

Starkey sits back on his bench.

STARKEY

Is he late?

MARGARET

She is.

Starkey looks at her oddly. He lifts a can, shakes it so that she can see there is a little left in it, and offers it to her.

STARKEY

Will you join me in a drink while you're waiting?

She looks at him as if to say, what an offer. *He takes the can and throws it behind him into the bushes.*

STARKEY

Absolutely right. It's pisswater.

She smiles, then removes the wine from her bag and unscrews the cap before pouring herself a papercupful.

MARGARET

It's okay, I've some wine here.

STARKEY

Wine. Is that what students are drinking these days?

MARGARET

What makes you think I'm a student?

STARKEY

The sophisticated screw-top bottle suggests you may not yet be in gainful employment.

MARGARET
(Laughs)

Well, maybe I am.

STARKEY

Studying what? Let me guess. Medical student? No – you didn't give me the kiss of life. But sitting all by yourself . . . accountancy? C'mon, gimme a break here. Farmer's daughter – agriculture? Horticulture? You can lead a whore to culture but you can't make her . . . Geology, sociology, archaeology, neurology, any sort of ology?

MARGARET
(Laughing, then cutting in)

Art, if you must know.

STARKEY

Art?
(Beat)

Why do art students not look out the window in the morning?

MARGARET
(Tuts and shakes her head)
So they'll have something to do in the afternoon.

*She looks back up the path for her friend, then back to Starkey,
then at the ground.*

Good gravel, was it?

He gets up, crosses over to her and sits down.

STARKEY
Do you know, it's easy to take the piss, but there's a lot
you don't know about gravel. By the way –
(extends his hand)
– Dan Starkey.

MARGARET
Oh, I know who you are.

STARKEY
Seriously?

MARGARET
Seen your column in the paper.

STARKEY
Laugh a lot, do you?

MARGARET
Better than the other shite.

STARKEY
'Better than the other shite.' Put that on my gravestone.

10

Margaret laughs, then there's an awkward silence. She nods at the crate of drink.

MARGARET

You're not seriously going to drink all of that yourself?

STARKEY

It's for a party. I was just thinking, seeing as you don't appear to have any friends, would you care to join me? My crowd. My music. My house . . .

MARGARET

Your crowd. Your music. Your wife.

STARKEY

You really do read the columns. I'm impressed. How's about it?

MARGARET

She wouldn't mind you turning up with a pretty young thing like me?

STARKEY

It's a party! Parties need people. Besides, she trusts me. And I don't mess around.

MARGARET

Aye, 'less you get the chance.

STARKEY

C'mon . . . live dangerously.

MARGARET
(Looks at him for a moment)
Aye, all right then. What've I got to lose but my
reputation?

STARKEY
That's the girl.

*He starts to pick up the carry-out as she gets her bags together. He
paints the scene.*

We'll go through the door, the place'll be swinging.
Patricia'll be waiting to greet us on the Magic Settee.

MARGARET
(She stops)
You have a magic settee?

STARKEY
It's not *magic* magic. We, uh, call it that because most
times we sit on it we end up making love.

She gives him a look.

We haven't sat on it for a while.

INT. STARKEY'S HOUSE – NIGHT

*We see Patricia sitting on the Magic Settee, cradling a drink. The
camera pulls back to show a throng dancing to punk music. Many
of them are wearing album covers on their heads; an explanation
of this is not necessary.*

*Patricia doesn't look particularly thrilled to see her house
transformed into a punk gig.*

Mouse is dancing extravagantly, but stops as he sees something and hurries out of the room.

As Dan and Margaret approach the lounge, Mouse heads them off. His voice is naturally loud and deep.

MOUSE

Whataboutcha, Big Man, and . . . and . . .
> *(wagging a finger)*

. . . and this must be your cousin . . . ah, Mary now, is it?

Starkey puts his hand out to introduce her, then realises he doesn't know her name.

STARKEY

Ah. Oh.

MARGARET

Margaret . . .

STARKEY

Margaret . . . Mouse. Mouse . . . Margaret. Mouse, outta the fuckin' way . . .

He laughs, then pushes on past into the lounge. Margaret raises her eyes apologetically.

MOUSE

Dan! She's not in the best of form . . .

Margaret waits in the doorway, with Mouse beside her.

MARGARET

So why do they call you Mouse?

13

MOUSE
(Bending down to her ear)
BECAUSE!

Dan emerges from the crowd to sit beside Patricia. She ignores him. For a moment they both watch the dancing, then continue to look ahead as they talk.

STARKEY
So. How's married life treating you?

PATRICIA
Been better.

STARKEY
Guy that owns this house says this is a magic settee. Sit on it, you end up making love.

PATRICIA
I think I'll go and get a drink.

She begins to get up, but he puts out a hand and pulls her to him; they kiss. She pushes away from him.

STARKEY
Guy that owns this house says –

PATRICIA
Don't even think about it.
(He laughs)
Working late, were you?

14

STARKEY

Someone has to.

A new song, something by The Clash, starts. Starkey looks towards the dance floor, keen to dance.

PATRICIA

Who's the wee girl?

STARKEY
(Shrugs, still looking towards the dance floor)
No one. Just bumped into her coming up the road. Margaret something.

PATRICIA

You're always picking up bloody strays.

STARKEY

It's care in the community.

An album cover suddenly crashes down on his head. He laughs, and is dragged towards the dancing.

PATRICIA

And just the one. You usually manage a couple.

STARKEY

Hey – from now on, my feet do the talking. C'mon!

She shakes her head as he is swallowed up by the dancing. We soon see him pogo-ing merrily.

He tries to make his way back to Patricia, but he's grabbed and hauled back in. Patricia laughs, shakes her head, and drinks.

15

We see from Starkey's POV as he begins to get the spins. He staggers as he leaves the room.

INT. STARKEY'S HOUSE – KITCHEN – NIGHT

Starkey steadies himself in the kitchen doorway. Margaret is kneeling in front of the fridge. She removes a large bottle of cider.

> MARGARET
>
> Cider. Brilliant. Two bottles of this and you wake up with a pile of vomit in your slippers and six hours pregnant.
> > *(Beat)*
>
> Are you okay?

Starkey nods, then bolts suddenly for the stairs.

INT. STARKEY'S HOUSE – BATHROOM – NIGHT

Starkey is throwing up in the toilet. He breathes hard, then throws up again. He reaches up, pulls the chain, then rests his head on the ceramic bowl.

Mouse appears in the doorway

> MOUSE
>
> Y'alright?

> STARKEY
>
> Yeah . . . yeah.

> MOUSE
>
> Do you want me to get Trish?

Breathing hard, Starkey pushes himself back from the bowl.

STARKEY

No. No thanks.
> *(He takes a couple of deep breaths)*

Right. Second half.

MOUSE

Then shift yourself. I'm dying for a pish.

Starkey gets to his feet.

INT. STARKEY'S HOUSE – STUDY – NIGHT

Margaret is standing in Starkey's study. The door is open and the room is lit only by the light from the hall. She is running her fingers along the spines of books. She lifts one out and looks at it.

STARKEY
(o/s)

A lot are review copies. From the paper.

Starkey is standing in the doorway.

MARGARET

It's rare you get macro-economics and a biography of Skippy the Bush Kangaroo in the same collection . . . Feeling better?

Starkey enters the room, takes the book from her and replaces it. They are now very close. Neither makes an effort to move. We hear the toilet flush in the background and feet going down the stairs.

STARKEY

My mouth tastes like a horse's arse.

17

MARGARET

You want a mint? My last one.

She smiles up at him, and we see a mint jutting out of her mouth. She raises her eyebrows in invitation. Starkey bends to take it. His teeth close on it. She isn't letting go. They're both smiling, and, in a second, they're both kissing, the mint still somewhere in-between them.

This would be quite erotic if he hadn't just been sick.

PATRICIA

You have twenty-four hours to move out.

Starkey turns, panicked.

Patricia's in the doorway, surprisingly calm, but her eyes are steely. She suddenly turns for the stairs.

STARKEY

Patricia . . .

He tries to go after her, but Margaret holds on to him.

MARGARET

That was nice . . .

STARKEY

I'm in trouble. I have to go.

He removes Margaret's arm and hurries quickly after Patricia.

EXT. BELFAST STREET – NIGHT

Margaret and Starkey are standing beneath a street light. It's not quite clear what they're doing until we close in. Starkey's face is bloody; Margaret wipes at his nose.

18

MARGARET

As I believe the song says, the best part of breaking up is
when you're having your nose broken.

(Beat)

Will you keep still?

STARKEY

Well, then, stop friggin' pokin' me.

*She laughs, shakes her head, then takes him by the arm and leads
him across the road.*

MARGARET

C'mon. My place isn't that far away.

STARKEY

Nah . . . Look, seriously, I should go back.

MARGARET

I'm not having a murder on my conscience. Just for a
while. Till Lizzie Borden calms down. Anyway, I thought
you didn't mess around . . .

STARKEY

I don't . . .

MARGARET

Or just never been caught.

STARKEY

I'm tellin' ya . . .

(v/o)

I had never considered being unfaithful, or at least not

19

with anyone I had any remote possibility of getting. Fantasy is the justifiable preserve of the married man.

INT. MARGARET'S HOUSE – NIGHT

Margaret and Starkey hit the floor in Margaret's living room.

Music is playing, something fast and furious, as they tear at each others' clothes.

Margaret suddenly stops and holds him off.

> MARGARET
> *(Breathless)*

You gotta have one . . .

> STARKEY

I don't. I'm married . . .

> MARGARET
> *(Desperate)*

Oh, God!

He is still touching her. It is definitely going to happen.

> STARKEY

I could use my sock.

> MARGARET

And not only would I have a baby, but it would come out wearing a little jumper. Oh, God . . .

She grabs him to her. They begin to make love. It's fast and passionate.

MARGARET

Promise me you'll withdraw. Promise me you'll
withdraw. Promise me you'll withdraw!

They both come. Explosively.

MARGARET

You . . .

STARKEY

We British don't withdraw from Ireland.

INT. MARGARET'S HOUSE – NIGHT – LATER

*They're lying back, naked, on the carpet of the lounge. They smile
at each other. Margaret rises to her knees.*

MARGARET

Fancy something to eat?

*Starkey nods and smiles as she steps over him. He looks up as she
opens the kitchen door, then looks about the room. There's a
photograph of Margaret with a young man, and one of her father
and mother.*

MARGARET
(o/s)

Authentic Italian pizza okay? I can zap it in the
microwave.

STARKEY

Fine. Who's the –

*He turns towards the kitchen. A Jack Russell's bared fangs are
inches from his face. He's growling.*

21

STARKEY
(Weakly)

Help.

The teeth move a little closer . . . and then the dog is suddenly yanked away.

Margaret, still naked, is holding the dog under her arm. It licks her face.

MARGARET

Sorry. This is Patch. His bite's worse than his bark. Isn't it, son? He must like you, or he'd have torn your throat out.

Starkey rubs at his throat as Margaret takes the dog back to the kitchen.

STARKEY

Who's the . . .

His voice is high-pitched, still scared. He clears his throat. More manly now.

Who's the photo of? Brother? Boyfriend?

MARGARET
(o/s)

My first real boyfriend.

We hear the pinging of the microwave. Starkey stands and lifts the photo down.

STARKEY

Long over?

MARGARET
(o/s)

Long enough.

STARKEY

But still has a place in your heart . . .

Margaret comes through the door carrying the pizza on a plate. She turns, pushes Patch back into the kitchen with her foot and closes the door.

MARGARET

I should take it down. Sentimental . . .

STARKEY

He looks a bit . . . Should I know him?

MARGARET

Patrick. Patrick Keegan.

STARKEY

Cow Pat Keegan?

Margaret nods, bashfully.

God! I kissed the mouth that kissed the mouth of Cow Pat
Keegan.

MARGARET
(Takes the photo and looks at it)

Don't worry. He's not going to come gunning for you.
He's in prison.

STARKEY

God. Cow Pat Keegan. I thought he looked . . . The
Paper Cowboy: thirty-three bank robberies for the IRA,
and he gets done for cattle rustlin' on the bendy word of
a supergrass.

MARGARET

Anyway, are you going to eat this?

STARKEY

Cow Pat Keegan. King of the Congo. Public enemy
number –

*Still looking at the photo, Starkey lifts a slice of pizza and bites
down. A sound not unlike that of a small building collapsing
issues from his mouth.*

MARGARET

I think I might have had it in too long.

STARKEY

No . . . no . . . Jesus, it's like eating a discus. I'm
sorry . . .
                    (They smile)
I suppose I'd better get going.
                    (Margaret nods slowly)
Although public transport at this time of night is rarely
dependable.

INT. STARKEY'S HOUSE – DAY

*The front door opens and Starkey enters, his face a mask of false
joviality, like they've just had a minor tiff.*

24

STARKEY

Hello! Casanova's home!

There is no response. As he walks through the house we see that it is in a bad state. There are beer cans everywhere, albums scattered about the floor and ashtrays full to overflowing.

He sees the red light blinking on the answerphone and presses play while he goes and opens the fridge.

PATRICIA
(v/o)

Hi. Only me. Hope you had a nice time with the wee tart. I've gone away for a few days. Please leave me alone. We're having too many fights. Drinking too much. We should think about what we want.
(Beat)
A man called Parker called, asked you to meet him at the Europa. Oh, and you know your mint condition copy of the Sex Pistols' *Anarchy in the UK* you say is worth £300? I melted it under the grill. Byeee . . .

Starkey slams the fridge door shut and charges for the cooker. He pulls out the grill and finds a mess of plastic.

STARKEY

Oh, for Jesus sake.

He turns away, looks at the kitchen, the rest of the house. It feels empty and cold. He sighs.

STARKEY
(v/o)

What is it that makes us treat our loved ones like shite, but perfect strangers like royalty?

INT. NEWSPAPER OFFICE – DAY

Starkey crosses the busy newspaper office. Mouse is on the phone; he waves Starkey over, but Starkey raises a hand – he has something to do first.

He takes a seat before his computer, lifts the phone and dials. As he waits for a response he removes a dart from the nose of the large photo of Michael Brinn on the wall of his work station.

A sub-editor, Paul, stops at Mouse's desk.

> PAUL
> *(To Mouse)*
> I need a piece of single column.

> STARKEY
> I bet that's what your wife says, too.

> PAUL
> At least my wife speaks to me.

Starkey gives Mouse a dirty look, then gives his attention back to the phone as his call is answered.

> STARKEY
> Hiya, Joe. Could I speak to Patricia?

INT. PATRICIA'S PARENTS' HOUSE – DAY

Joe, Patricia's father, is on the phone. It is a well-to-do house. Patricia is poised at the bottom of the stairs, beaten to the phone.

When Joe speaks there's not much warmth in his voice.

JOE

Yes, Daniel, just hold on.

He holds out the receiver to his daughter and gives her a look. She takes it and holds it against her chest, giving her hovering father the eye.

He retreats into the kitchen and closes the door.

INT. NEWSPAPER OFFICE – DAY

Mouse, still on the phone, is trying to indicate to Dan to put his phone down. Dan winks back and ignores him, master of his own destiny . . .

STARKEY
(To Patricia)

Hi. Are you okay?
(Beat)
It's no use nodding on the phone, you have to actually make a noise.

PATRICIA
(o/s)

You're not funny, Dan.

STARKEY

I think you'll find most of my readers disagree.

PATRICIA
(o/s)

Most of your readers don't have to live with you.

27

STARKEY

C'mon, Trish. Some girl tried to kiss me. You beat me up, I walked the streets. I'm sorry. Come on home.

PATRICIA
(o/s)

It's not as simple as that, Dan. You do something like that, it puts up a wall between us. It can be impossible to get over.

STARKEY

They got over the Berlin Wall. They pulled it down.

INT. PATRICIA'S PARENTS' HOUSE – DAY

Patricia is on the phone; a tear appears in her eye. It slowly rolls down her cheek but Starkey can't see it and can't tell from her voice.

PATRICIA

Did you sleep with her, Dan?

INT. NEWSPAPER OFFICE – DAY

Starkey is still on the phone, his voice quieter now. Mouse puts his phone down and hurries across to him.

STARKEY

Of course I didn't sleep with her! I was bleeding everywhere. I went round to Mouse's to get patched up –

He looks up to see Mouse making a cutting motion across his throat. Realising he's put his foot in it, he rolls his eyes and his head flops back. Mouse shrugs and turns away.

28

Then Starkey is stunned by a sudden broadside from –

                              WOODS
Are you going to get any fucking work done today?

Starkey puts the receiver to his chest.

                              STARKEY
It's a source, okay?

                              WOODS
Aye, source of the fucking Nile. Get your finger out, for
fuck sake.

Woods exits. Starkey lifts the phone again.

                              STARKEY
– but Mouse . . . must have been asleep, I couldn't . . .
Trish, I – Trish? Aw, for Jesus . . .

He puts the phone down and looks across to Mouse.

                              MOUSE
She called first thing, wanting to know if I'd seen you.

                              STARKEY
Fuck.

                              MOUSE
Shouldn't mess around with the wee dolls, Dan.

                              STARKEY
Thanks, Mouse, I'll bear it in mind.

                              MOUSE
Aye, and I hope you bear it in mind you're meant to be
seeing that American guy –
                         (looks at watch)
– thirty-five minutes ago.

                            STARKEY
Fuck . . .

EXT. BELFAST STREET – DAY

Starkey climbs into the back of a taxi.

*At first he can't see the driver because her head barely comes up
past the headrest. She peers round the seat. She's tiny, but with a
crew cut, cap-sleeve T-shirt and a cigarette hanging out of her
mouth; she's hard as nails. She can't be much more than a
teenager, but could pass for fifty on a bad night.*

She scowls at him.

                            STARKEY
Europa Hotel.

*She nods, an inch of ash falls from her cigarette, then pulls out into
the traffic, nearly causing a crash. She yells out the window:*

                            DRIVER
Fuck away off and die!

*Starkey slumps back in the seat. The driver looks at him in the
mirror.*

                            DRIVER
Starkey? That's some fuckin' crap you write in the paper.

                               30

STARKEY

Thanks.

DRIVER

Mind you, the husband loves it.

STARKEY

Good.

DRIVER

But then, he's a stupid fucker.

STARKEY

I see.

DRIVER

But not stupid enough to drive a fuckin' taxi, that's for sure.

STARKEY

No.

DRIVER

Gets me to drive the fucker 'cause he's scared ah gettin' fuckin' topped. So he sits at home worryin' about me . . . Like fuck. The fuckwit. Down the fuckin' pub.

STARKEY

Uh-uh.

31

EXT. EUROPA HOTEL – DAY

Starkey gets out of the taxi and pays through the window. As we follow him into the hotel we hear car horns from behind and shouting.

> DRIVER
> *(o/s and distant)*

Fuck away off!

INT. EUROPA HOTEL – DAY

Starkey approaches the reception desk. A young woman smiles at him.

> STARKEY

Hi, I'm supposed to be –

> PARKER
> *(o/s)*

Dan Starkey?

Starkey turns.

A very large black man with receding hair and wearing a smart suit and trench coat stands before him. He has a newspaper folded in his hand.

Starkey looks genuinely surprised.

> STARKEY

Uh-uh . . .

32

PARKER

Charles Parker. *Boston Globe.*

They shake hands.

STARKEY

Sorry I'm a bit late.
                    (Looks at his watch)
Bomb scare. C'mon up then . . .

He turns towards the lifts and Parker follows.

INT. ELEVATOR – DAY

Starkey and Parker stand at the back of the elevator while the attendant gives Parker a very strange look.

There is country-and-western Muzak playing in the background.

STARKEY

Don't take it the wrong way. There really are no black people in Northern Ireland. Plenty of Orange, plenty of Green. He –
                    (nods at the lift attendant)
– expects you to take out a machete and cut his nose off.

PARKER

I've eaten already.

The lift attendant's head turns very slightly towards them.

INT. CONFERENCE ROOM – HOTEL – DAY

An election press conference is underway. Lots of reporters, cameras and party workers. On the platform, standing before a UN Peace Flag, is Michael Brinn.

33

He's in his early forties, well groomed, attractive with a flashy smile, oozing charisma.

REPORTER
(A young woman)
You were recently voted sexiest man in Ireland by *Northern Woman* magazine. How does your wife feel about that?

BRINN
(Mock embarrassed but actually loving it)
Oh, gosh – you'll have to ask her that. I'll tell you one thing, I don't feel very sexy after a twelve-hour meeting discussing European fish quotas.

Laughter from the press.

Cut to Starkey looking at Brinn, while Parker, his back to the stage, fills his face with sausage rolls from a buffet table as the conference continues.

STARKEY
(Addressing Brinn)
You changed your name when you entered politics. Don't you think that you've in some way betrayed your Catholic heritage by dropping the 'O' prefix from Brinn?

There's a chorus of low groans from the assembled reporters.

BRINN
No, I think maybe I just have a vowel problem.

The reporters burst into laughter. Starkey is stuck for a response while Brinn goes on the offensive.

BRINN

I simply believe that in this country too much stock is
put in your prefix. The fact that I had an 'O' at the start
of my name automatically meant that I was disliked and
distrusted by certain Protestants.

(He opens his hands and spreads them like Jesus)
I am just a man, a man who wants peace. The less
pre-conceived notions I carry with me, the less prejudice
I will have to overcome. That's what we all want, isn't it?
Peace?

*There is a smattering of applause. At the back of the hall, Starkey
remains unconvinced.*

STARKEY

Look at that, the reporters are applauding. Jesus.

*Parker shrugs and opens a bottle of beer; there are pastry crumbs
around his mouth. He drinks.*

PARKER

Seen one evangelist, seen 'em all. I predict a landslide
victory.

STARKEY
(Shaking his head)
If he bottled that charisma he could sell it as hair oil.

PARKER

I've read the file. You'd have to be a heel not to vote for
him.

*Parker puts down his bottle of beer. He looks serious for a moment
and Starkey awaits something profound.*

PARKER

Tell me one thing.

(Beat)

What's the difference between Bush whiskey and Black Bush whiskey?

Starkey looks at him for a moment, then gives a little laugh.

INT. EUROPA HOTEL – DAY

Starkey and Parker come through the double doors. At the top of the stairs there are two men talking. One of them, Alfie Stewart, is facing Starkey and is in animated conversation.

STARKEY

Alfie, how're ya doin'?

Stewart stops talking and nods hello. The other man, Billy McCoubrey, turns around. He's a huge man in a too-tight suit. Starkey's jaw drops.

STARKEY

(Rapid fire and walking quickly past Billy)

How's the form, can't stop, must go, catch ya later . . .

He takes the steps one at a time, but extremely quickly; Parker makes a confused, half-apologetic gesture to Stewart and McCoubrey and hurries after him.

McCoubrey leans over the banister and shouts after him:

McCOUBREY

I haven't forgotten, ya wee shite!

EXT. EUROPA HOTEL – DAY

Starkey emerges from the revolving doors, stops, and looks back nervously. Parker appears behind him.

PARKER

What was that all about?

STARKEY

C'mon.

He leads Parker out towards Great Victoria Street, their sights set on the Crown Bar across the road.

STARKEY

The big fucker's a UVF warlord. That's Protestant militia to you. Trouble is, elephants and Billy McCoubrey never forget. I wrote something sarky about

38

him a couple of years ago. Guys like that don't sue. But there was a phone call, and for some months I didn't sleep. When I went out, I wore a big hat.

They approach the bar.

PARKER

And the other guy?

STARKEY

Alfie Stewart. Brinn's right-hand man.

PARKER

And what would they be doing together?

STARKEY

Arguing, like everyone else in this stupid friggin' place.
>   *(Beat, as Starkey opens a swing door)*
Your round, mate.

INT. CROWN BAR – DAY

Starkey and Parker are at the bar. Before them are lined up half a dozen glasses each, most of them empty. Starkey points at the glasses.

STARKEY

Right, four outta four. You won't make five.

Parker raises a glass, swirls it round, takes a little sniff then downs it in one.

PARKER

Jamesons. Tastes better in Ireland.

39

STARKEY
(Raises his glass and downs it)
That's Northern Ireland, Mr Parker. Or Ulster, if you're a
Protestant. The Six Counties or the North of Ireland, if
you're a Catholic. If you're the British Government, you
call it the Province.

PARKER
And what do you call it, Mr Starkey?

STARKEY
I call it home, Mr Parker. After you.

PARKER
(Downs one)
Now that's Black Bush.

STARKEY
Son of a bitch.
(He lifts his glass and tilts it at Parker)
Here's to peace in our time.
(He drains it)

PARKER
(Drains his next one)
Plain old Bush.
(Beat)
He was injured in a bombing, wasn't he?

STARKEY
Brinn? Aye. The IRA tried to blow up a police dinner,
but it was double booked. The Cavalier King Charles
Spaniel Club's annual shindig got blown to hell. They
were pickin' bits of Fido out of the trees for weeks.

Thirteen people died. Brinn got badly burned.

                    PARKER
And that's how he got started.

                    STARKEY
Aye, the sympathy card.

                    PARKER
He still play it?

                    STARKEY
Only to gullible Yanks.

*He smiles, then lifts two glasses at once and pours one into the
other.*

And then there are the fine blends.
                    (He drains the glass)

EXT. MARGARET'S HOUSE – DAY

*We see Margaret approach her front door, but from POV of a
surreptitious 'watcher' behind a car. She lets herself into her house
with a key; there is a newspaper sticking out of the letter box which
she has trouble removing. She closes the door.*

*We see her pass a window then the 'watcher' changes position so
that when we see Margaret again she is standing in the lounge
with the paper open.*

INT. MARGARET'S HOUSE – DAY

*Margaret is standing by the window, reading the paper. There's a
large picture of a smiling Michael Brinn on the front. She's*

chuckling. We swing round to see Dan's photo at the top of his column.

Suddenly, the window explodes inwards. Margaret screams, is showered with glass and dives to the floor. She covers her head. There's another explosion and more glass.

She begins to crawl forward, then encounters a small, round object. She grasps it and looks perplexed.

> MARGARET

Potato?

There is another explosion, but more distant. Margaret stands suddenly and looks out of the window.

> MARGARET

Oh, God.

EXT. MARGARET'S HOUSE – DAY

Patricia is standing in the middle of the road, a bag of potatoes at her feet and a potato in each hand. She throws one and scores another hit on an upstairs window. Then she sees Margaret looking out.

> PATRICIA

If you want to fuck him, you can cook for him as well.

She fires another potato, this time at Margaret, who has to dodge out of the way as it smashes through another part of the window.

> PATRICIA

And I'll be back tomorrow; he just loves turnip.

*With one final throw, Patricia turns and hurries to a Renault car
parked nearby. There's a cold fury burning on her; she has shed
that tear.*

EXT. MARGARET'S HOUSE – NIGHT

*Starkey climbs out of a taxi. As he turns away from the car he
stops suddenly and looks up at the house. All but one of the
windows are boarded up and that one is still being worked on by
two men in overalls.*

> STARKEY

Oh, Patricia . . .

INT. MARGARET'S HOUSE – NIGHT

*Margaret is showing him the damage. There's hammering in the
background.*

43

MARGARET

I thought someone was shooting at me.

STARKEY
(Throws a potato up and catches it)

Comber spuds. If I know Trish, she'll have shopped
around for the best deal. Who're the guys outside?

MARGARET
(shrugs)

My dad organised them. He came round with my
birthday present. Nearly had a coronary.

STARKEY

Happy birthday.

MARGARET

Aye, hold your horses. It's not for another fortnight.
Except Daddy's going to be busy, so he brought it round
early . . .

*She lifts an oblong gift-wrapped box and gives it a shake. She
laughs and begins to tear off the wrapping.*

Every year he tries to instil a little culture in me. Hear that?
Hear the old bones rattling?

*Starkey steps forward and looks at a large boxed set of cassette
tapes.*

STARKEY
(Reading)

Orchestral Magic, An A–Z of Classic Composers. Mightn't
be that bad.

(He turns the box slightly)
Recorded by the National Orchestra of Azerbaijan.

Margaret runs her fingers along the line of tapes, then pulls one out.

MARGARET

Here. D for Dan. From me to you. A present for coming to save me.

Starkey takes the tape from her and looks at it.

STARKEY

I'm . . . speechless. No one's ever given me one-twenty-sixth of their birthday present before . . .

MARGARET

If you think it's any good, come back for the rest.

STARKEY

You just want me to come back twenty-five more times.

She smiles and slips her arms round his waist and kisses him. After a long moment, he pulls clear. She begins to kiss his face, all over.

STARKEY

I love her.

MARGARET
(Still kissing him)
What're you saying?

STARKEY

I'm just telling you: what ever happens between us, I love my wife.

She looks up at him and she has that look in her eye that first snared him.

Maybe you can love two people.

She puts a hand to his face, then runs a finger down his chin on to his chest and down out of sight. As she does, we see the eyes of the two workmen, just above the ledge, watching.

INT. MARGARET'S BEDROOM – NIGHT

They are lying in bed together silently, his arm around her, looking at the ceiling. They turn and look at each other and we think from the intensity of their gaze there must be a Big Thought on the way, but:

STARKEY & MARGARET
(Simultaneously)

Chips.

They laugh.

EXT. BELFAST STREET – NIGHT

Starkey is hurrying along the street in the rain. He comes to the chip shop and tries the door, but it's locked. He stands back and reads a hand-written sign on the door: CLOSED DUE TO VARICOSE VEINS.

STARKEY

Oh, for Jesus . . .

He turns back into the rain, looks further up the street then hurries on.

INT. PIZZERIA – NIGHT

Starkey is standing with his forehead pressed against the window of a pizzeria. A guy and girl in red-striped uniforms are flirting behind the counter. Starkey looks at his watch, then back to the staff. There is a public phone on the wall. He lifts the receiver and dials.

STARKEY

Joe, is Trish there? No. It's okay. Yeah, everything's fine.

He puts the phone down just as the boy behind the counter puts a pizza on the counter.

STARKEY
(Lifting it and leaving)

About bloody time.

47

PIZZA BOY

Hey, sometimes you gotta wait for quality.

(Beat)

And sometimes you gotta wait for shite.

The boy and girl giggle.

Starkey pauses in the door, thinks about saying something, then walks on.

EXT. MARGARET'S HOUSE – NIGHT

Starkey is hurrying along with the pizza, sheltering the box from the rain under his coat. As he approaches Margaret's house he sees that the door is already half open.

INT. MARGARET'S HOUSE – NIGHT

Starkey enters the house, which is in darkness.

STARKEY

Hey! Pizza man's here! Come on down!

He pushes open the lounge door, puts the light on and stops. The lounge has been torn to pieces: records are scattered everywhere, the settee is sliced up. The box of tapes is gone, but only the eagle-eyed would notice.

He drops the pizza.

STARKEY

Margaret!

He charges back out into the hall and disappears up the stairs.

INT. MARGARET'S ROOM – NIGHT

Starkey enters Margaret's room at a rush. The light is on.

STARKEY

What the hell's going –

We can see Margaret's naked back, then she turns slowly in the bed. She pulls the white bed sheet tight around her. Starkey thumbs back down the stairs.

STARKEY

I don't believe you slept through . . .

As he watches, the sheet begins to turn red. Within moments, it is soaked.

STARKEY

Oh, Jesus Christ.

When she speaks, her voice is bubbled, like she's drowning.

MARGARET

Dan . . . Dan . . .

He rushes to the bed and is about to grab her but as the pain shoots through her and she grimaces and freezes up, he hesitates . . .

STARKEY

Jesus Christ. Margaret . . . please . . . God . . .

MARGARET

Dan. Divor . . . Divor . . .

She's in agony and waves him closer.

49

STARKEY

Doctor . . . I'll call a –

She grabs him with a bloody hand.

MARGARET

Divor . . . ce . . . divorce . . . Jack. Divorce . . .

STARKEY

Don't, Margaret . . . please . . .

*He hugs her to him. He is covered in blood, but it doesn't matter;
she's dying. She finally goes limp in his arms. We see Starkey's
face: he is crying. Slowly he sets Margaret back down on the bed.
He looks at her, then reaches across to close her eyes. Suddenly,
her body is wracked by the final death rattle which is absolutely
spine-chilling.*

*Starkey staggers back from the bed towards the door. Then,
finding that his legs simply won't support him, grabs at the door
for support, slowly sinks to his knees then lies down. He stares at
the bed, almost comatose. A tear appears in his eye and rolls down
his cheek.*

*We hear a creak – Starkey's eyes shift towards the door – then
another creak. He rears up to his knees. He is panicked. He has
spastic, jerky movements. He doesn't know what to do: he's
helpless and scared witless. A killer is approaching.*

*He looks back at Margaret, dead on the bed, and suddenly the
anger wells up in him. He charges out of the bedroom and throws
himself on the approaching figure and they go thumping down the
stairs. We see Starkey bounce free and hit the front door.*

He sits for a moment, stunned, then scrambles to his feet.

STARKEY

Come on then, you fucker! Get the fuck up!

He runs at the motionless form and gives it a bloody good kick.

C'mon, you murdering bastard!

He stands with fists clenched, ready to die, ready to fight, ready to cry, but there is no response from the supine figure. He approaches cautiously, then rolls the figure over with his foot. We can't see the figure clearly. Starkey kneels and puts a hand out to feel the figure. We hear a shattered –

STARKEY

Oh, God.

INT. MARGARET'S LOUNGE – NIGHT

Starkey enters the lounge. He bends and picks up the pizza, straightens it in the box, then walks towards the kitchen. He's in a daze and reverting to type: he needs food and alcohol.

He opens the kitchen door and suddenly Patch barks rabidly – shocking Starkey. Breathing hard, he sticks out a finger and screams:

STARKEY

You fuckin' move, I'll kill you!

Patch stops barking, lies down and puts his head between his paws.

INT. MARGARET'S LOUNGE – NIGHT – LATER

Starkey and Patch are sitting on the settee together. Starkey is eating pizza and drinking from a bottle of vodka. He is still staring vacantly ahead.

STARKEY

(v/o)

I sat and thought of lovely Margaret. Of her hair and her eyes and her laugh and the way she kissed me and her skin that smelt of mandarin oranges. I had heard the last words she would ever speak, she had died in my arms. What would she think of me now? Would she still love me now that I had pushed her mother down the stairs and broken her neck?

INT. MARGARET'S HALL – NIGHT

Margaret's mother is lying, wide-eyed and with her neck broken, at the bottom of the stairs.

INT. MARGARET'S BEDROOM – DAY

Light is just seeping through the cracks in the boards that cover the windows in Margaret's bedroom, giving an eerie effect.

Margaret's body is covered by the bloody sheet, but her hand hangs out over the side. Starkey is asleep beneath the hand, an empty bottle of vodka beside him. Patch is curled up at the bottom of the bed, also asleep.

The clock radio by the bed shows it is 7.59 a.m. in red numbers. At 8 a.m. the radio suddenly comes on with 'Something Else' by Eddie Cochrane (or a similar rock'n'roll number – 'She's sure fine lookin' man, she's Something Else').

Starkey shoots up out of his sleep and, when his face hits the hand, screams and shuffles back; Patch barks madly from the side of the bed.

STARKEY
Shhh . . . Shhhhh . . . It's okay, it's all right.

Patch quiets down. Starkey lifts the sheet back, looks at Margaret and shakes his head.

It's all right.

INT. MARGARET'S HOUSE – DAY

Starkey and Patch descend the stairs. Margaret's mother lies white and stiff, open eyes staring, at the bottom. Starkey steps carefully over her. He opens the front door a fraction and peers out.

EXT. MARGARET'S HOUSE – DAY

A milk float passes by; otherwise, the street is quiet.

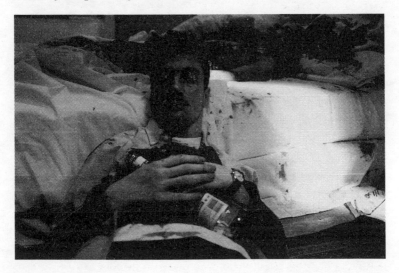

INT. MARGARET'S HOUSE – DAY

As Starkey turns from the door, he finds Patch sniffing at Margaret's mother's body. He kicks out at the dog who yelps and races out the gap in the door.

EXT. MARGARET'S HOUSE – DAY

The front door opens and Starkey slips out. Patch runs off up the road.

Starkey pushes a hand through his hair, pulls his jacket tighter about him and begins to walk. It is suddenly busier. There are people going to work, mothers pushing babies, kids with schoolbags; he looks fearfully at them, convinced that they know. A car horn sounds and he jumps. We hear his exaggerated heartbeat.

INT. STARKEY'S HOUSE – DAY

Starkey is shaving, watching himself in the bathroom mirror. He cuts himself by mistake, and is traumatised as he watches the blood drip down his chin.

STARKEY
(v/o)

Where was Patricia? Could she have done it? Would she have done it? Hell hath no fury like a woman scorned . . .

INT. STARKEY'S HOUSE – DAY

Starkey is sitting at the top of the stairs. He's wearing a dressing gown and staring into nothingness.

STARKEY
(v/o)

Who's Jack? Why's he getting divorced? What am I
doing? Go to the police. Someone killed Margaret. I
killed her mum. Jesus Christ, I –

*There is a sudden hammering on his front door. He looks down.
He sees the outline of a large man in the smoked glass. Behind
him, there is a light flashing, like on a police car.*

*Starkey sits for a minute, then he raises his hands, joins the wrists
together as if they have been handcuffed and walks down the
stairs. The hammering on the door continues. He opens the door.
Parker is standing there. Across the road, there's an ice cream van
with a flashing light serving local kids.*

PARKER

Hey, Mr Starkey, we've a cancellation. Ready to meet the
next Prime Minister?

EXT. BELFAST – DAY

*Parker is driving Starkey to their appointment with Michael
Brinn. Starkey is silent. As Parker drives, there is Northern Irish
country-and-western music on the radio. He sings along with it in
an exaggerated good ol' boy manner. Then he laughs.*

PARKER

You guys are really into all this shit.
(Beat)
One phone call, they say come on in and meet the man.
They must be really desperate for dollars.

STARKEY

Yeah.

Parker punches a button on the radio, and another C & W record comes up. Then another button and another C & W song.

PARKER

Shit.

(To a sick-looking Starkey)

You okay, man?

STARKEY

Hangover. Discussing politics with Mr Smooth isn't going to help.

PARKER

And I thought you could drink. Man, you were walking sideways. C'mon, Starkey, you gotta give the man a chance, you've been fighting each other for so long you've forgotten –

STARKEY

(Snapping)

And what the fuck would you know about it?

(Beat)

Sorry.

(Sighs)

Sure, thirty years of it, then oilskin comes along with a full set of teeth and some trendy platitudes and everyone thinks, how refreshing, let's vote for him. But he's not any different, he's just got better marketing.

PARKER

You're a cynic with a hangover. Isn't he uniting Protestants and Catholics?

STARKEY

Aye, and who was the guy who united gunpowder with
matches? Okay, I just don't think you can please all of
the people all of the time and still run a fucked-up
country like this. Forgive and forget is a nice concept, it's
just not very realistic.

PARKER

What were you drinking last night?

He presses another button and we hear more country and western.

Fuckin' radio. Shoulda brought my own tapes. Thought I
was coming to a land of music and culture. Fuckin' Jim
Reeves.

*Starkey gives a grim laugh, feels his jacket pocket then removes a
tape and pushes it into the cassette player.*

STARKEY

If it's culture you want . . .

*Parker lets out a great guffaw and slaps the wheel. As he does, the
tape begins to spill out of the cassette player.*

*Starkey removes the tape, puts one of the cassette holes over his
little finger and begins to spin it round, rewinding the tape. Parker
hits one of the radio buttons again and a different country-and-
western tune comes on.*

PARKER

Fuckin' Jim Reeves.

EXT. RED HALL – DAY

Parker's car enters the wrought-iron gates of Red Hall, and is waved through by a security guard after the briefest of checks. The car moves up the driveway towards an impressive seafront house.

INT. RED HALL – DAY

Parker and Starkey are being led down a long, dark corridor by Alfie Stewart, Brinn's right-hand man and head of security. He is a big man and looks like a bouncer.

> STEWART
> So how's it going, Starkey? Still the leading graduate of the smart-mouth-can't-write school of journalism?

> STARKEY
> You got it, Alfie.

Stewart knocks on the door.

INT. STUDY – RED HALL – DAY

The study doors open and Alfie leads Parker and Starkey into a book-lined room. Michael Brinn is standing by a window, looking out. Alfie indicates that the journalists should sit, then takes up position behind them, leaning against the door.

Brinn turns around slowly. He looks at Parker and raises a hand in an electioneering pose.

> BRINN
>
> If you're an honest worker, I've been there too! If you're unemployed, I've been out of work too! If you're disabled, I haven't been there yet, brother, but if you don't elect me, I'll shoot myself in the foot!

Parker looks stunned, Starkey grins sheepishly and Brinn laughs out loud. We see now that he has a newspaper in his hand. He holds it up to Parker.

> BRINN
>
> I take it from your reaction that you're not familiar with young Mr Starkey's work.

He walks forward and extends a hand to Starkey.

> Dan. At last. I'm a great fan.
> *(Moving to Parker)*
> And Mr Parker. You don't know what you're missing.
> *(Beat)*
> *Boston Globe*, isn't it?

> PARKER
>
> Yes, sir . . .

BRINN

By way of a trade union paper in Cleveland and a weekly
political journal in Washington . . .

PARKER

You've done your research, too.

Brinn takes a seat and folds his hands in front of him.

*Parker produces a tape recorder and sets it on a coffee table that
sits between them. He lifts a notebook and begins flicking through
it looking for his questions.*

BRINN

Oh, it pays to be up to scratch on our American cousins.
Spirit of Watergate and all that. Besides, it was either
you or some Albanian eejit with barely a word of
English. So fire away. Hit me with your hardest first, if
you like, then we can relax and have some tea.

PARKER

Do you believe in capital punishment for murder?

Starkey looks up, stunned.

BRINN

For terrorists?

PARKER

All murder is terrorism.

BRINN

But not all terrorism is murder.

PARKER

Are you playing with words or answering questions?

BRINN

I'm playing with questions.

This isn't quite the PR job Brinn was looking for. He switches the emphasis quickly to Starkey.

BRINN

You know what my party's policy on capital punishment is, don't you, Dan?

Starkey makes a high-pitched choking sound and just manages to nod.

Parker isn't deflected.

PARKER

So even though you were badly scarred in a bomb – what is it, twenty per cent burns . . . ?

BRINN

Thirty.

PARKER

Thirty . . . You're not bitter?

BRINN

Of course I'm bitter. Bitter that we've let this go on for thirty years when with a little guts we could have sorted it out.

PARKER

You still in pain?

61

BRINN

What?

PARKER

The burns.

BRINN
(Tuts)
I really would like to get away from this.

PARKER

But why? Surely it's the single most –

BRINN
(Fighting to keep his anger in check)
Mr Parker, look at me. I've prospered. I'm about to become
Prime Minister. But there are a lot of orphans out there. A
lot of widows. My people have been dying for thirty years.
(Pointing the finger)
It. Stops. Now.

*Brinn expects that to be the emotive end to it, but Parker ploughs
on.*

PARKER

It just worries me that this is being built up as some kind
of Utopian state, all forgiveness and light . . . But in
practice, if you get elected and the Brits pull out, what's
to stop the Protestants or the Catholics starting the whole
war up again? Their cease-fires have never lasted . . .

STEWART
(Pushing himself off the door)
Because if we're elected and they try causing trouble,
we'll have the mandate to deal with it. And the balls.

PARKER

Are you suggesting a military crackdown?

BRINN

No! No. Ach, lighten up. What we've got now is the feel-good factor you Americans love in your movies. The happy ending. All I'm saying is give peace a chance.

PARKER

Didn't they shoot John Lennon? Okay, say the Irish-American lobby started making demands and threatened to stop pumping money into your campaign unless you promised an amnesty for Republican terrorists?

Starkey leans back and closes his eyes. We hear:

MARGARET
(o/s and distant)

Promise me you'll withdraw . . .

INT. BEDROOM – MARGARET'S HOUSE – NIGHT

Margaret is on the bed, the blood rapidly soaking through the covering sheet.

INT. STUDY – RED HALL – DAY

Starkey runs his hands down the front of his shirt, lost in his own world.

BRINN

Dan . . . Dan!

Starkey suddenly comes awake.

63

STARKEY

Oh . . . Jesus . . . Yes, sorry . . . I'm sorry. I'm feeling a
bit . . . Sorry, I need some fresh air . . .

*Starkey jumps to his feet, staggers slightly and hurries to the door.
Alfie Stewart opens it for him and gives a slight shake of his head
as Starkey hurries out, holding his mouth.*

EXT. RED HALL – DAY

*Starkey walks across the grounds of Red Hall. He looks out to sea,
opens his mouth and takes great gulps of the air. He's pale and
looks wretched.*

*A child's scream suddenly rends the air. Shocked and panicked –
he's been through too much already – Starkey looks about him
and looks like he might run away. The child screams again.
Starkey hurries forward to the low wall in front of him. He jumps
on to it and we see that the level of the land drops away below it.*

*There's a child on the ground, screaming, with a figure hunched
over him.*

STARKEY

Hey!

*The figure turns: it's Agnes, a woman in her late thirties with no
make-up (she doesn't need it), short hair and soft features. She is
wearing old green-stained clothes for gardening. The child, Robert,
screams again, and the scream dissolves into laughter. There are
two Cavalier King Charles Spaniels running about.*

STARKEY

Sorry, I thought . . . Sorry.

AGNES

We're only messing around.
> *(Starkey turns to step off the wall)*

It's Dan Starkey, isn't it?

She rubs her muddy hands on her trousers and hurries forward to shake his hand.

I'm a big fan.

She runs a hand through her hair.

STARKEY

Mrs Brinn.

AGNES

Agnes. Please. And this is Robert. Your meeting all finished?

STARKEY

No. Fresh air, I wasn't feeling –

AGNES
> *(Laughing)*

Hangover, is it?

STARKEY

Bad pint.

AGNES
> *(Smiles)*

Youse are staying for lunch, aren't you?

65

STARKEY

I'm not sure. No one said.

AGNES

'Course you are . . . C'mon up to the house, we'll see how things are going. Robert, come on!

She begins to lead Starkey back towards the house. Robert runs up beside Agnes.

AGNES

So are you as bad as you make out?

STARKEY

How do you mean?

AGNES

Oh – drinking, womanising, causing trouble . . .

STARKEY

I'm fond of drink, women, and stirring the pot. I don't think that makes me a bad man.
(Beat)
Unless I meet a drunk woman anarchist, then I'm lethal.
(He blinks, thinking: lethal)

AGNES

I'm safe then.

STARKEY

Oh, I wouldn't go that far.

She stops and looks at him.

Are you flirting with the wife of the next Prime Minister of Northern Ireland?

Starkey smiles and walks on.

STARKEY

Well, that depends on how the voting goes.

She laughs and walks after him.

We hear the sound of a police siren, distant at first, then louder as we see the first of a fleet of police vehicles turn into the driveway and race up towards the house, blue lights flashing and alarms ringing.

Starkey and Agnes hurry towards the house. The doors of the police cars burst open and heavily-armed police clatter out with Starkey and Agnes caught in the middle. She pulls her son up into her arms and Starkey begins to raise his . . . then slowly lowers them as he realises they aren't after him; they are taking up positions around the front of the house.

The main doors of the house open and Alfie Stewart emerges, followed by Brinn, fixing his tie. Agnes rushes up to him.

AGNES

Michael, what . . . ?

He puts a hand on her shoulder. He looks shaken.

BRINN

Agnes, love . . .

Stewart puts a hand on Brinn's shoulder and whispers something. Brinn looks at Starkey.

BRINN

No, it's okay, they'll know soon enough . . . David
McGarry, our Economic spokesman. His wife Edna and
daughter Margaret have been murdered in Belfast.

AGNES

Oh, Jesus!

Brinn hugs her to him. Starkey looks stunned.

BRINN

I know . . . I know . . .
(His voice starts to break)
Is there no depth to which they . . . ? I'm sorry, love, I
have to go.

*He stands, then leans down and kisses Agnes on the top of her
head.*

AGNES

Is there anything I can —

BRINN

Be strong. Believe.

*He nods at Starkey and then Alfie leads him across to the police
cars. The cops move behind them and get back into their vehicles.
The convoy moves off, sirens blaring, leaving Agnes and Starkey
alone.*

Agnes has her hand over her mouth, shaking her head.

AGNES

God . . . I just can't . . . Only yesterday . . .

There's hurried footsteps and Parker appears in the doorway, still doing up his trousers.

PARKER

Go for a crap and World War Three breaks out . . .
What the fuck's going down, Starkey?

Starkey shakes his head and bites on his lip.

EXT. ROAD – DAY

*Parker and Starkey are driving along a dual carriageway.
Starkey stares ahead: he looks like he's on speed, his mind is racing and his hands are drumming on his legs.*

Parker's excited, but keeping a close eye on the mirror. C & W music is on the radio.

PARKER

Did they say what part of Belfast?
(*Starkey shakes his head*)
You're the local . . . C'mon, man, liven up! At last a decent angle . . .

Starkey gives a grim laugh.

STARKEY

It's all over.

PARKER

Damn right it is! If Brinn holds this together, he deserves to get elected. But who would've done it? IRA, breaking their cease-fire? The Protestants wanting Britain to stay in –

69

                         STARKEY
Or just a lone nutcase . . .
         (He sees Parker looking in the mirror again)
What's wrong?

                         PARKER
I have an idea we're being followed.

                         STARKEY
Aye.
                  (He starts to turn)

                         PARKER
Don't make it so obvious.

*Starkey rolls his eyes, then slumps in his seat, turning slightly
back. We see three cars coming up behind them on the dual
carriageway.*

                         STARKEY
Two reds and a white. Which one?

                         PARKER
Not the Jap. Not the Yugo. The Fiat.

Starkey turns back in his seat.

                         STARKEY
Either way, it's a sad reflection on the British car
industry.
                      (Beat)
Relax, you're not that important.

The rear driver's side window explodes.

PARKER

What the fuck?!

The car veers sharply to the left as a shocked Parker tries to regain control. There's a great thud and the car shakes as it mounts the grass verge at speed and careers along it before Parker manages to swing it back on to the road.

There's another shot and the rear window shatters.

PARKER

Jesus!

(*Ducking down*)

Who are these guys?

STARKEY

You can interview them later – just fucking drive!

We see the car in pursuit. There are four men inside: one of them, a skinhead, is hanging out the front passenger window, firing a pistol. Several times the cars crash together with various bits falling off. Parker, it becomes clear, is no slouch in the driving department.

Another bullet yings through the front window. We see the skinhead with the gun laughing his head off. He has something written on his forehead. The cars are racing towards a roundabout, with a bus coming from the right. Parker's car just squeezes past but the bus catches the rear of the pursuit car and spins it round. As it comes to a halt, the driver tries to start the engine, but it stalls.

Parker stops the car.

71

What the fuck are you doing?

Parker smiles and throws the car into reverse .

PARKER

Hey, I'm from New York. We do this for breakfast.

The car speeds backwards. The driver is just climbing out of the other vehicle as Parker's car smashes into it, crushing him. There are other screams from within.

STARKEY

Jesus Christ!

Parker drives forward again, his car now much the worse for wear.

PARKER

Now that feels better.

Starkey looks at him, aghast, then begins to brush splinters of glass off his jacket.

EXT. STREET MARKET – DAY

The car is chugging past Bangor's open-air market when it finally gives up the ghost and rolls to a halt. They sit, staring out of the front window. Music in background is C & W.

PARKER

Tell me that was a simple carjacking.

STARKEY

That was a simple carjacking.

Parker slaps the steering wheel.

PARKER

What the fuck is going on here, Starkey? I go to the john, two people get murdered, then someone tries to run me off the road. My stories are good, they're not that fucking good.

STARKEY

They weren't after you.
                    (Beat)

PARKER

Don't be so fucking cryptic. If you know –

STARKEY

They were Protestant paramilitaries.

PARKER

How could you tell?

STARKEY

One, they fucked up. Two, the gunman had FTP written on his forehead.

PARKER

FTP . . . ?

STARKEY

Fuck The Pope. Actually, they're getting better. Usually they can't spell FTP.

PARKER

But why would they –

STARKEY

I don't know!

Parker shakes his head and tries to calm Starkey down.

PARKER

Okay. Listen. All I know is my car's been shot up. I gotta call the cops.

He starts to get out of the car.

STARKEY

You can't call the police.

74

PARKER

I have to.

STARKEY

Please!

Parker stops. He sits back in his seat, takes out a packet of cigarettes and offers one to Starkey. Starkey shakes his head. Parker lights up.

STARKEY

Have you ever done anything really, really stupid?

PARKER

I have the feeling I might just be about to . . .

EXT. MARKET – DAY

Starkey and Parker are in the middle of a busy open-air market. Starkey stops by a pay phone and begins searching his pockets.

PARKER

But why didn't you know?

STARKEY

Aye, you're making love to a beautiful woman and you're thinking, I wonder if she's a famous politician's daughter.

PARKER

There must have been clues! Her name, her –

STARKEY

I didn't know her name! I wasn't meant to be there . . . It just happened.

PARKER

You think those guys were after you? Revenge or . . . ?

STARKEY

Yes. No. I don't fucking know.
                    (Beat)
Have you got any change?

Parker pats his pockets and shakes his head.

PARKER

American Express . . .

Starkey tuts and replaces the telephone receiver. He crosses over to one of the market stalls which is selling second-hand CDs and tapes. A lazy big sod sits behind the counter reading a paper. There is a radio playing C & W.

STARKEY

Afternoon.

The Sod barely looks up; he thumbs at a sign taped to the top of his stall: SORRY, NO CHANGE FOR THE PHONE.

STARKEY

I want to sell you a tape.

Starkey shows him the tape, the Sod takes it, gives it the briefest of looks and hands it back.

SOD

Sorry, no demand for crap like that.

STARKEY

I'm only looking for a pound.

76

SOD

Keep looking.

STARKEY

50p.

SOD

Deal.

Back at the telephone, Starkey starts punching some numbers.

PARKER

Call the police, Starkey. Do yourself a favour.

STARKEY

Would you?

They look long and hard at each other. Parker slowly shakes his head.

STARKEY
(Into the phone)

Hi, Joe, is Patricia there?

JOE
(o/s)

Sure, Dan . . . Hold on.

STARKEY
(To Parker)

I just need a bit of time.

JOE
(o/s)

It's Daniel, love . . .

INT. PATRICIA'S PARENTS' HOUSE – DAY

Patricia takes the phone from her dad, then waits for him to retreat; he waits. She raises her eyebrow; he gets the hint and disappears into a different room.

Patricia takes a deep breath, then puts the receiver to her ear. She has turned slightly now, so that she's facing the smoked glass front door of the house.

PATRICIA

Okay, okay! Before you start. She was askin' for it.

EXT. MARKET – DAY

We see Starkey blanch at her apparent admission, then falteringly:

STARKEY

You really . . .

PATRICIA
(o/s, cool, almost callous)

They do say revenge is a meal best served cold.

Starkey's face seems to collapse. His wife has murdered Margaret . . .

INT. PATRICIA'S PARENT'S HOUSE – DAY

Patricia is on the phone. We see a figure appear at the front door.

78

So I potatoed her.

She smiles, but of course Dan can't see this. It's suddenly quite a warm and loving smile.

STARKEY

Not the potatoes! For fuck sake, Trish, I'm talking murder and you're talking garden vegetables! Did you fuckin' –

PATRICIA

Will you stop shouting! Now what are you –

There is a heavy thump on the front door. Patricia looks up. She can see a figure through the glass panel. She tuts.

PATRICIA

Dad!
                    (Tuts again, then to Starkey)
Just hold on a second.

She sets the phone down and begins to move towards the door, but the glass is suddenly shattered and a man in a balaclava, wielding a pick axe, steps through. He is quickly followed by four other men carrying guns.

EXT. MARKET – DAY

Starkey is on the phone with Parker lolling nearby. A scream so loud issues from the receiver that Starkey drops the phone in shock and steps back.

STARKEY

Jesus Christ . . .

He steps forward and picks the phone up again.

STARKEY

Patricia? Patricia? Patricia!

Passing shoppers are staring. He slams the phone down and looks panic stricken.

PARKER

What's –

STARKEY

Shut the fuck up!

He stabs his finger at the phone, dialling 999.

OPERATOR
(o/s)

You have dialled the Emergency Services. Which service, please?

STARKEY

Every fucking service!

Cut to:

INT. BOARDING HOUSE – NIGHT

We see a lamp shade behind which are caught two moths, silhouetted. The lamp flashes on and off. In the moments of light we see a rundown room in a rundown boarding house in a rundown area of Belfast. The wallpaper is from the sixties, the ambience by Nico Teen. From above we see Starkey lying on a single bed, staring at the ceiling, switching the light on and off.

INT. BOARDING HOUSE – DAY

Starkey is fully dressed, asleep on top of the bed. There is a sudden knocking on his door. He jumps up, panicked. He moves cautiously to the door, then shouts without opening it:

> STARKEY
> I'm in the shower. Can you clean it later?

> PARKER
> I don't intend cleaning it at all. Open up, Dan, you sound like a scared rabbit.

> STARKEY
> *(Opening it)*
> I am a –

He is confronted by a large photograph of himself, dominating the front page of his own newspaper. It is colour and badly printed, but Starkey nevertheless. He staggers back.

Parker, still hidden behind the paper, speaks in clichéd, hard-boiled newsman style:

> PARKER
> Journalist sought in McGarry murder sensation!

Parker drops the paper. Behind him we see doors with numbers on them; it is clear it is a small hotel or guest house.

Parker gives Starkey a sardonic smile.

STARKEY

For Jesus sake, don't do that to me.

Parker enters the room. He is carrying a plastic bag which Starkey ignores for the meantime, instead he rips the newspaper off Parker and paces the floor, reading it.

STARKEY

Jesus – I didn't . . . How could they . . . No fucking way
. . . Jesus, I work with these guys. What about Patricia,
what do they –

PARKER

Page three. She's missing. Her parents were bound and
gagged.

Starkey turns to page three, reading maniacally.

STARKEY

Missing, how can she be? I mean, don't they . . .
            (Sighs)
I have to find her. I have to find out what the fuck is
going on.

PARKER

I had a chat with the police. They don't seem to know
much either.

STARKEY

You went to the –

PARKER

They came to me . . . They're rather embarrassed that a
double murderer was allowed such easy access to the

next Prime Minister of Northern Ireland. I told them you
hadn't said a thing, and I hadn't seen you since I
dropped you off downtown yesterday.

STARKEY

They believe you?

PARKER

Doesn't matter. They're still looking for you. Here.

Parker hands Starkey a bag. Starkey opens it and peers in.

STARKEY

Ah ha!

*Starkey pours the contents of the bag on to the bed. He produces a
pair of jeans, a denim jacket and a blonde wig. He holds it out
with considerable distaste.*

Parker smiles and goes to peer out the window.

STARKEY

You're not serious.

PARKER

There was a charity shop three blocks down. You wanted
a disguise, best I could do. They said it came from a
dead woman.

STARKEY
(Smelling it)

Did they scalp her?

83

He puts it on and goes and looks at himself in the mirror.

> STARKEY

Jesus.
> *(He takes it off)*

This isn't going to work.
> *(Beat)*

Were you able to . . .

> PARKER

I spoke to some of Margaret's classmates at college. She used to have a friend called Jack.

Starkey peers down at the legs of the jeans.

> STARKEY

They're slightly flared.

> PARKER

Jack's a civil servant by day; by night he becomes Giblet O'Gibber, a stand-up comic. He's at the Dolphin Hotel tonight.

> STARKEY

Well, he must know more about this than I do, 'cause I know fuck all squared in a box.

> PARKER

Shit . . .

Starkey looks up at Parker, who steps to the side of the window.

It's the Fashion Police.

EXT. BOARDING HOUSE – DAY

Four police Land Rovers have drawn up outside. Heavily-armed policemen are assembled outside, getting their final instructions from an inspector. With a nod, he turns and leads some of them up the steps into the boarding house, others move towards the back of the hotel.

INT. BOARDING HOUSE – DAY

Starkey stashes his new clothes in a bag and prepares to run.

> STARKEY
> If you make it, the Dolphin at eight, okay?

Parker runs left while Starkey kicks in the door on the right.

INT. BOARDING HOUSE – DAY

Starkey enters a bedroom. There are two nude, fat, middle-aged men sitting on Spacehoppers.

> STARKEY
Afternoon.

He races to the window, peers out, pulls it open and climbs out. He freezes as the police pass by beneath him.

INT. BOARDING HOUSE – CORRIDOR – DAY

Police come crashing along the corridor just vacated by Starkey, kicking in doors. They come to Starkey's room.

INT. BOARDING HOUSE – STARKEY'S ROOM – DAY

The door bursts open. Three heavily-armed NIPD officers crash through the door.

Parker has his back to them, fixing his tie in the mirror. Without looking round he says:

> PARKER
> *(Nonchalantly)*

Just leave it on the table.

INT. DOLPHIN HOTEL – NIGHT

It is a seedy-looking lounge of a Belfast hotel. A country-and-western singer on a small stage is murdering a classic. From behind we see a long bar: most patrons standing at it face the singer; one woman, with blonde hair and denims, faces away from the action. We switch round to see her. It is Starkey, with the wig on.

The camera roves around the lounge showing tough guys relaxing at the bar while their hatchet-faced wives bitch at their tables. Mutton dressed as lamb is the order of the day: smart suit sleeves are rolled up to display tattoos and that's just the women. The laughter is loud and raucous. The women have big perms, like an explosion in a mattress factory; the blokes have big Mexican bandito moustaches.

> STARKEY
> *(v/o)*

Even terrorists have to socialise. Every once in a while they succumb to ghetto madness and break out into the city, and this is where they come. Both sides. They exchange pleasantries, broker deals, identify targets.

Look, there's the IRA arguing the finer points of their Marxist philosophy. And the UVF debating the football results.

The country-and-western band are saying thank you and goodnight.

(o/s)

Ladies and gentlemen, a big Dolphin welcome, please, for Giblet O'Gibber!

There is loud applause and cheering. A balding comic in a dinner jacket ambles out on to the stage. He's odd-looking with a comedian's face: like he was beautiful when he was born, but the midwife put her hands in his mouth and stretched it sideways.

He approaches the mike and takes it off the stand.

GIBLET

Evening. I hate fuckin' bouncers. Who the fuck do they think they are?

The audience is already laughing loudly.

And I especially hate bouncers in up-market fucking hotels. Sorry, mate, no denims. No denims! Fuckin' wise-up. This is Belfast! My mate was wearing Denim aftershave, they weren't going to let him in. My other mucker, Denis, had to argue with him for half an hour, finally let him in as long as he changed his name to Bernard.

INT. TOILETS – DOLPHIN HOTEL – NIGHT

Starkey is at the urinal. He finishes, zips, turns and bumps into a huge man. It is Billy McCoubrey.

STARKEY
Oh, sorry big lad, didn't see ya.

He hurries past. McCoubrey, brow furrowed, looks after him, half recognising him . . .

INT. DOLPHIN HOTEL – NIGHT

Starkey is back at the bar, nervously sipping his pint. A hand clamps down on his shoulder and he jumps and turns.

It's Parker.

PARKER
Sorry I'm late, I –

STARKEY
(Hissing)
Fuck off! Just watch who you're fucking pushing . . .

Starkey rolls his eyes, trying to get a surprised Parker to move off . . .

> PARKER
>
> I was only –

> STARKEY
>
> You lookin' fuckin' decked?
> *(Quieter)*
> McCoubrey's watching us, I'll call you later.

Parker nods. He raises his hands apologetically and moves up the bar.

Meanwhile, Billy McCoubrey is looking at Starkey, trying to place him. Beside McCoubrey is the hood from the car chase with FTP tattooed on his forehead. The tattoo is hidden by an Elastoplast and he has his arm in a sling.

> GIBLET
>
> In case you haven't heard the sad news, three IRA terrorists were killed earlier this evening when their car left the road and hit a tree in West Belfast.
> *(Beat)*
> The UVF said they planted it.

There's a pause while the terrorists try to work out whether they've been insulted, then they follow McCoubrey's lead as he begins to laugh.

Starkey sets his drink down and slips through the stage door.

INT. DOLPHIN HOTEL – CORRIDOR – NIGHT

A door opens on to the corridor and Giblet O'Gibber comes through to the sound of applause. He is wiping his face with a towel as he walks and has a bottle of beer in one hand. He comes to a door, opens it, enters and is about to close it when Starkey appears in the doorway.

STARKEY

Jack? I wondered if I could have a word.

GIBLET

My manager's downstairs.

He slams the door in Starkey's face.

INT. HOTEL ROOM – NIGHT

There is another knock on the door. Giblet opens it angrily.

STARKEY

Comedy is easy. Dying is hard.

He punches Giblet in the face and Giblet goes tumbling across the room. Starkey follows, shaking his fist in pain at the same time.

He closes the door and locks it.

STARKEY

Good manners don't cost anything, Jack.

GIBLET

What the fuck was that for?

STARKEY

That was for nothing.

Starkey kicks him in the stomach. Giblet reels back.

STARKEY

And that was for Margaret.

Giblet is coughing on the floor. Starkey stands over him.

GIBLET

Margaret. Whaddya —

STARKEY

Why'd you have to kill her, Jack?

GIBLET

Who the fuck are you?
                    (Starkey kicks him again)
Jesus Christ . . . it wasn't me! It was that cunt Starkey!

Starkey's on his knees. He pulls Giblet up by his collar.

STARKEY

I am Starkey, you stupid bastard! The last thing she said
on this earth was about you!

*The emotion is welling up in Starkey now; he throws Giblet to the
carpet again and stands up. He walks across the room.*

Jesus Christ, man, why'd you have to kill her . . . ?

GIBLET

I swear to God I didn't . . . I haven't seen her for weeks.
                    (He pulls himself up to a sitting position)
What did she say . . . about me?

STARKEY

She was dying. She said Jack. Jack. And Divorce.

GIBLET

Divorce? What does that have to do –

STARKEY

I don't know! I'm trying to find out!

There is a knock on the door. Starkey turns towards it. Then another knock, louder.

McCOUBREY

(o/s)

Giblet! Open up!

And then suddenly Giblet is on Starkey's back, pulling him backwards, raining blows into his face. They tumble to the ground and wrestle on the floor.

The banging on the door is now thunderous.

GIBLET

It's Starkey! It's Starkey!

Starkey manages to get on top of Giblet. He thumps him. The door shudders under the weight of a boot. Starkey, panicked, gets off Giblet and hurries to the window; he pulls it up and looks out. Something shakes him: Giblet has grabbed his legs.

GIBLET

It's him! I've got him!

The door comes off its hinges, falling inwards. McCoubrey fills the doorframe. Starkey kicks free of Giblet and climbs out of the window. McCoubrey and several heavies rush into the room.

92

EXT. HOTEL – NIGHT

Starkey clings to guttering on the side of the hotel. As he tries to climb further along, the guttering gives way and he falls, landing on and going through the roof of a parked 2CV. Inside, several panicked dogs begin to attack him. He throws himself back out of the car, lands on the ground and rolls. He gets to his feet and begins to limp away.

McCoubrey is framed in the window upstairs.

McCOUBREY

Starkey! After him!

INT. HOTEL – NIGHT

The C & W band is back on and the hoods are up dancing. McCoubrey's men pick up their guns from behind the bar and charge through the dancers towards the exit.

EXT. HOTEL – NIGHT

Starkey is moving as fast as he can across the car park. As he reaches the busy Great Victoria Street, the hotel doors burst open and McCoubrey's men come rushing after him, guns drawn. Night-time revellers scream and scatter as McCoubrey's men begin to fire.

Starkey scrambles through the crowd, the hoods in hot pursuit. He moves off the pavement into the traffic, dodging cars. The gunfire continues; a bullet catches him in the leg and he tumbles to the ground.

He drags himself to his feet. A Mini screeches to a halt, stopping just a couple of inches from him. Starkey leans on the bonnet as he moves round to the passenger door and wrenches it open. There is a nun sitting behind the wheel.

STARKEY

In the name of God, help me!

NUN

Fuck away off!

A bullet yings over Starkey's head. The nun yelps. He tumbles into the passenger seat.

STARKEY

Drive!

Another bullet shatters the rear driver's window. The nun takes off at top speed, then looks in the mirror to see if they are being followed.

STARKEY

Thank you, Sister.

NUN

You can stick your sister up your hole.

Starkey is touching his leg. When he raises his hand to his face it is covered in blood.

NUN
(Tuts)
And bleeding all over the friggin' car.

Starkey leans back, closes his eyes, then opens them and turns his head towards the nun. He's alive and slightly exhilarated by the fact.

STARKEY

Do you mind me asking which particular order you're
from? You strike me as more Armalite than Carmelite.

*The nun is driving, but looking anxiously at Starkey's leg. She
shakes her head, pulls up her habit and pulls down her stocking,
which she throws into Starkey's lap.*

NUN

Tie the fucking thing, try and stop the flow. The Royal
Victoria is just –

STARKEY

I can't go to hospital.

NUN

You'd rather bleed to death?

STARKEY

I can't go!

NUN

(A big sigh)

Go on. Tell me you're a terrorist. Tell me. I've spent the
night being felt up at a priest's retirement party, now I've
a gunman dying in my front seat.

STARKEY

I'm not a terrorist. My name is Dan Starkey. I am
wanted for two murders I did not commit. I am being
chased by the IRA, the UVF, the RUC and the British

Army. My wife has disappeared and I've just given a
rather good comedian a hiding and been shot in the leg
for the privilege. Please help me, Sister.

NUN

I'm not a fucking nun!

*She glares across at him, but as she does Starkey's head tumbles
forward, banging off the glove compartment.*

He's unconscious.

Oh, for Jesus' sake . . .

INT. NUN'S APARTMENT – DAY

*Starkey is just waking up. He's naked in the bed. The nun is
buttoning herself into a nurse's uniform. We can see now that she's
young, early 20s, with short, dark hair.*

*Starkey's wig sits on a chair beside the bed. He looks at her
blurrily for a moment.*

NUN

I'm afraid I had to amputate.

*This knocks the fog from him and his hand races to his bandaged
leg. He winces.*

NUN

Relax. It's just a flesh wound. You've lost a little blood. I
stitched you up . . . Yes, nun-o-gram by night, nurse by
day . . . I'm sure you know what the health service
pays.

Starkey examines his bandaged leg, then lies back on the bed and stares up at the ceiling.

NUN

Your picture is plastered all over the papers.

She lifts a newspaper and tosses it on to the bed. Starkey looks at it warily.

NUN

And the funerals. And that girl you didn't kill, her dad's had a heart attack. He's on a life-support machine.

STARKEY

It just gets better and better.
(Beat)
Thank you for not turning me in.

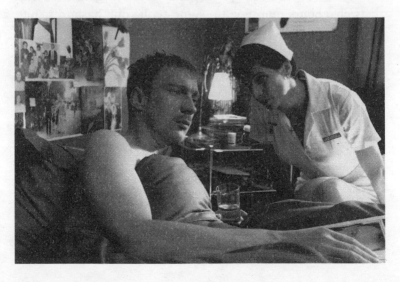

NUN
(Shrugs)
I used to read your stuff in the paper. They think you've
kidnapped your wife.

STARKEY
Aye, sure. She's in my back pocket.

NUN
I'm only telling you what they –

STARKEY
I know. I'm sorry.
(He smiles)
I know who you are. You're Florence Nightingale.

NUN
Aye, and Florence Nightingale is about to spend the next
twelve hours mopping up some senile oul' bastard's shite.

STARKEY
Right now, I'd love that job.

NUN
Aye, I had to do yours last night 'n' all.

She has her coat on now and is ready to leave.

STARKEY
Oh.

*She smiles and walks towards him. She pulls the covers up over
him.*

NUN

Rest. I'll see you later.

STARKEY
(Wearily)

What do I call you? Sister? Nurse? Florence?

NUN

Lee. Lee Cooper.

STARKEY

You're serious?

NUN

Unfortunately, yes. My parents thought they'd a sense of humour.

He smiles and his head lolls back on the pillow.

STARKEY

Lee. If you were me, what would you do?

NUN

I'd crawl into bed and pull the covers up over my head. I'd sleep until the nightmare was over.

STARKEY

Do you think that would work?

NUN

No.

She smiles and exits.

Starkey pulls the covers up over his head.

EXT. LEE'S FLAT – NIGHT

Lee is walking towards her flat. As she turns into the doorway a van drives past, plastered with Brinn posters and a megaphone booming:

> MEGAPHONE
> Vote Brinn for a new tomorrow. Vote Michael Brinn for your children's future . . .

INT. LEE'S FLAT – LATER

We hear the sound of a key in the door and Lee enters her flat. Starkey is sitting on the edge of the bed, phone in hand. His bandaged leg is stretched out in front of him.

> STARKEY
> . . . at eight. And bring your credit card.

He puts the phone down.

> LEE
> Just you be sure to leave 10p for the call.

> STARKEY
> Sorry, I –

> LEE
> Feeling better?

> STARKEY
> Yeah, I slept . . . I have to go, Lee. I have to see a man about a horse.

LEE

Well, I hope you buy it, you shouldn't be walking on that
leg.

She sets a bag on the bed.

I washed your jeans. Couldn't do much about the bullet
holes. I've another job on tonight. If you want, I'll give you
a lift.

STARKEY
(Pulling the clothes out of the bag)
Thanks. I'd be lost without you.

LEE

Aye.

*She moves towards the bathroom, unbuttoning her uniform as she
goes.*

INT. LEE'S FLAT – BATHROOM – NIGHT

*Lee's standing in her underwear before a large mirror, applying
make-up. She flips on the radio. We hear doomy classical
music.*

LEE

Did you hear the IRA have shot two Mormons in Derry?

STARKEY
(o/s)

Morons?

LEE

Mormons. Apparently they were mistaken for plain clothes police. It was the short hair and superior smiles.

INT. LEE'S FLAT – BEDROOM – NIGHT

Starkey is struggling into his jeans. He is lying back on the bed pulling the trouser leg carefully over the bandage.

STARKEY

Well, that's the end of that campaign. Once the Mormons are on their case, the IRA'll be begging for peace terms.
>   *(Beat)*
Jesus, haven't you anything more cheerful than that?

INT. LEE'S FLAT – BATHROOM – NIGHT

Lee stands up from the toilet, pulling up her knickers. She laughs.

LEE

What's wrong with –
>   *(flushes chain)*
Dvořák?

She pauses for a second and checks herself in the mirror again. Then moves to the bathroom door.

A little culture never did anyone –

INT. LEE'S FLAT – BEDROOM – NIGHT

Lee appears in the doorway.

LEE

– any har– Aaaaah!

She is grabbed from behind by Starkey and hurled on to the bed.
He dives on top of her. She tries to fight back.

LEE

Will you get the fuck off me!

STARKEY

Who're you working for? Who're you with?

LEE

Get off me!

He tries to pin her down, but she's bucking under him. He's falling
apart. He can't trust anyone.

STARKEY

What's going on? Who're you working for?

She's punching back at him.

LEE

I'm working for the fucking health service! Dan! What's
got –

He has hold of her hands now, pinning her down.

STARKEY

You said it, you said it . . .

LEE

Said what?

STARKEY

The last words Margaret ever said to me, and I never told you . . .

LEE

I didn't say a thing! I didn't mean anything!

She's crying now, scared, confused, still struggling . . .

STARKEY

Divorce, you said it, Divorce Jack . . . You said it . . .

LEE

Dvořák! The music! The bloody composer!

He stares at her, still thinking she's trying to trick him, fighting with himself.

The music on the radio comes to an end.

DJ
(o/s)

Ah, now . . . the only cheque I have that doesn't bounce . . . Dvořák . . .

Starkey sits back, stunned. Lee rolls up into a sitting position.

STARKEY

Oh, Jesus Christ! Dvořák, Dvořák! Oh, God, Lee . . . I've been so stupid. So obvious . . .

She swings out, slapping him across the face. He hardly feels it.

LEE

You ungrateful bastard . . .

STARKEY

Lee . . . I'm sorry, I –

LEE

I gave you the benefit of the doubt and then you just –

STARKEY

Lee. Listen to me . . . I'm sorry. Lee! I thought it was a person . . . Jack . . . but Dvořák . . . I thought you were in on it, but it's not a person, it's a tape, a friggin' classical tape!

She wipes tears from her eyes; he looks at her and shakes his head.

STARKEY

And I sold it for 50p.

EXT. BELFAST STREET – NIGHT

Lee's Mini, with the rear window taped up, drives through Belfast.

EXT. STREET – NIGHT

The car stops opposite an up-market restaurant. Lee is dressed as a nun; Starkey is in his denims and wearing the blonde wig.

Lee moves to turn the engine off.

STARKEY

Keep it running. They're not used to nuns round here, they're likely to throw boulders first and ask questions later.

105

LEE

I wasn't born yesterday.

STARKEY

Sorry. I keep thinking of you as a nun. Sheltered and virginal.

LEE

You'd be surprised.

They look into each others' eyes. Starkey is about to say something he will probably regret, but she cuts in.

LEE

I can wait for you if you want.

STARKEY

Does your life lack excitement by any chance?

106

LEE

I'd like to help. You've the world on your shoulders,
Dan, I can offer a shoulder pad to lean on.

STARKEY

You've done more than enough.

*He puts a hand on her shoulder, smiles, then leans across and
kisses her on the lips; he pulls away moments short of lingering.*

*There are two elderly women staring through the windscreen at
them.*

OLD WOMAN

The dirty baste.

*Starkey exits the car and closes the door. He turns and looks up at
the restaurant.*

The old woman hurries up.

OLD WOMAN

You're disgusting.

STARKEY

Fuck off.

OLD WOMAN

Fuck off yourself, cuntface.

*It stuns Starkey for a moment, then he hurries on to the
restaurant.*

Lee drives off.

INT. RESTAURANT – NIGHT

Starkey enters the restaurant, then pauses as he looks about for Parker. He spots him, but as he moves a maître d' stands in his way, looks at him snootily and raises his hand . . .

STARKEY

It's okay, I'm an artist.

He brushes past him, crosses the restaurant to Parker, then pulls out a chair at the four-seater table.

PARKER

Dan. How're you doing?

STARKEY

Fine. Once the bleeding stopped.

PARKER

I . . . hell, Starkey. You know the whole world's looking for you . . .

STARKEY

Yeah, I kinda guessed . . .

A figure appears at his side.

Oh, a bottle of Harp. Mr Parker?

But it isn't the waiter. The man pulls out a chair and sits. He has cropped hair, prematurely grey. Piercing eyes, square jaw, very well-dressed. There is a confidence about him, but it's not like Brinn's, it is altogether more chilling.

He puts out a hand.

KEEGAN

You'll be Starkey, then.

Starkey, confused, shakes. He looks to Parker.

PARKER

Sorry. I'd no choice.

KEEGAN

The name's Keegan. Pat Keegan.

STARKEY

Cow Pat Keegan?

Keegan nods, smiles, then winks across at the opposite table. Two hoods in suits nod back: they are Mad Dog and Frankie and are both Neanderthal in appearance. Mad Dog moves his jacket back to show a gun in a holster.

KEEGAN

My colleagues, Mad Dog and Frankie.

STARKEY

I thought you were in prison.

KEEGAN

I was. Released for good behaviour.

STARKEY

You still IRA?

KEEGAN
(Smirking at his friends)
Still? You think the 'RA wear suits like this? Now, don't
go feeling too badly about your friend letting you down.

*Keegan takes out a packet of cigarettes, removes one, puts it in his
mouth, then lifts a box of matches.*

We had a long game of Irish roulette this afternoon. I won't
go into the details, but it involved a petrol bomb in his
underpants . . .

*Keegan strikes the match, and Parker immediately blows it out.
He looks terrified.*

. . . and an ability to blow out matches.

*The waiter, a tall, imperious, balding chap, appears at the table.
Keegan picks up a menu.*

KEEGAN
By the way, Starkey, I understand you killed my
girlfriend.
(Beat)
Shall we order?

STARKEY
(Putting the menu down)
I'm not very hungry.

WAITER
Gentlemen, tonight our special is a breaded escalope of
turbot, which is prepared in a mixture of white bread
and brioche crumbs and served with a sorrel cream.

KEEGAN

Actually, we're in a bit of a hurry. A jam sandwich to go would be nice.

WAITER

We're really not that sort of –

KEEGAN

You have bread? You have jam?

WAITER

I see what you're driving at, sir, but –

The waiter stops suddenly as he feels Mad Dog's gun pressed against his groin. He turns back to Keegan.

WAITER

Raspberry or strawberry?

He hurriedly exits

KEEGAN

Now, I'd like you to tell me about the tape.

STARKEY

A tape?

KEEGAN

Now, let's not play stupid buggers. We both know about the tape. Just hand it over and we'll see what we can do for you that doesn't involve lead.

STARKEY

I'm sorry, but I've no idea what you're talking about.

KEEGAN

What a pity. But have it your way.

He stands up and pushes his seat back.

I do find that pain is such a marvellous memory stimulant.

EXT. RESTAURANT – NIGHT

Starkey and Parker leave the restaurant flanked by Mad Dog and Frankie, Keegan coming up behind. Keegan slides open the back of a gardening supplies minivan parked at the kerb and Starkey and Parker are ushered inside.

EXT. BELFAST – NIGHT

The van drives through Belfast. As it turns into a street we see a tall, brooding block of flats in the distance.

INT. VAN – NIGHT

Frankie is slabbering his way through one of the jam sandwiches. Parker and Starkey are blindfolded.

FRANKIE

Last fella we had didn't talk, we stuck the old blindfold on, took him up the Cavehill and shot him in the back of the head.

STARKEY

Why bother with the blindfold if you're shooting him in the back of the head?

FRANKIE

We wore the blindfolds! It was fuckin' amazin', took us twenty minutes to plug 'im.

112

INT. APARTMENT – NIGHT

We see Parker framed against a dark sky, looking very scared indeed. We pull back to see that he is standing on a window ledge, held in place by Mad Dog. Keegan, Starkey and Frankie stand in the lounge of a drab apartment. Mad Dog gives Parker a little push, but holds on to him.

PARKER

Jesus! Starkey, please . . .

STARKEY

I don't have the friggin' tape!

Keegan walks forward to Parker, and Mad Dog lets go of him. Parker is even more frightened, standing alone on the edge.

KEEGAN

His life is in your hands, Starkey. I'm going to make this

very simple for you. I am going to count to three. At the count of three, if you haven't told me where the tape is, Parker learns to fly. Okay?

(Starkey nods)

One.

PARKER

Starkey, tell him where the fuckin' tape is.

STARKEY

There's no point in this, I don't –

KEEGAN

Two.

PARKER

Starkey!

Starkey has held out as long as he can.

STARKEY

Okay! Okay. Stop it. The tape's –

KEEGAN

Three . . .

He pushes Parker off the ledge. There's no scream; he just disappears into the silent darkness. Starkey races forward, screaming, incredulous.

STARKEY

You bastard!

Frankie cracks him with his gun from behind, and Starkey tumbles to the floor.

Keegan grins and looks out the window after Parker.

KEEGAN

Fastest reader I ever knew. Thirteen stories in five seconds.

Starkey is crawling on the carpet, sick and stunned.

Which leaves us the small matter of the tape.

STARKEY

You can stick your fuckin' tape up your hole.

KEEGAN

I don't think it'd fit up mine, Starkey, but I know whose it might.

Keegan looks to Frankie and nods. Frankie turns and unlocks a bedroom door.

Starkey pulls himself up to his knees and rubs at the back of his head.

KEEGAN

Easy to be the tough guy in print, isn't it?
                    (Beat)
Ah, now . . .

Starkey follows Keegan's gaze and sees Patricia standing in the bedroom door. She's wearing a pink dressing gown and looks like she's been dragged backwards through a hedge. She smiles weakly at Starkey.

STARKEY
(To Keegan)

You fucker!

KEEGAN

Thanks very much for the offer, but I've done that already.

Starkey stands and looks at her oddly.

STARKEY

Trish?

Her tongue darts round the inside of her mouth, like it is looking for a way out. She stares at the ground. Starkey begins to step towards her, but stops, pivots, and plants a perfect punch on Keegan's nose. Keegan staggers back, bleeding.

Starkey turns back towards Patricia and we see from Starkey's POV the butt of a gun racing towards his face.

INT. BEDROOM – NIGHT

We see a dilapidated bedroom from above. Starkey and Patricia are lying very close together on a bed. As the camera moves in we see that they are tied up, face to face. Keegan has done it this way because he knows there will be a row.

Patricia is looking at Starkey, who coughs and begins to come out of unconsciousness. As we close up, we see an ugly bruise on his forehead. As they talk they begin to wriggle their way across the bed, their movements getting more desperate as their argument grows.

PATRICIA

. . . at long last. Like having a dead Siamese twin.

STARKEY

You . . .

(his forehead crumples as he tries to remember)

. . . you fuckin' slept with him!

PATRICIA

There wasn't much sleeping involved.

STARKEY

Oh, that's just lovely.

PATRICIA

Shits in glass houses shouldn't throw stones.

STARKEY

Or potatoes.

PATRICIA

I was at a low ebb. He cheered me up.

STARKEY

What, by kidnapping you? Jesus! I don't believe I'm
hearing this. I could understand if it was rape, but
this . . .

PATRICIA

You mean you'd prefer I was raped?

STARKEY

Yes! No! God, I don't know!

PATRICIA

It doesn't matter any more, Dan.

STARKEY

Of course it matters!

PATRICIA

It matters as much as you sleeping with her.

STARKEY

It's a different thing entirely! Okay . . . okay. It wasn't
right, and God knows I've, Jesus, she's paid for it . . . But
screwing someone who kidnaps you . . . Jesus.

PATRICIA

It happened to Patty Hearst.

STARKEY

You're not fucking Patty Hearst. You haven't got any
fucking money for a start.

PATRICIA

It hasn't crossed your mind I might be doing it for
revenge? To get even?

STARKEY

And how would I ever have found out? Don't make me
laugh. He's a fuckin' killer. What do you think he is,
Robin fucking Hood? He just pushed a really good man
off a balcony out there.

PATRICIA

He does what he has to, to survive.

119

STARKEY

It has nothing to do with survival! It was murder for the sake of it, and you screwed him!

PATRICIA

Ugh!

She's had enough, she pulls hard to one side and the shift in weight topples them off the side of the bed. They land with a thump, with Starkey on top of her.

STARKEY

Jesus, will you take it easy!

PATRICIA

Then just shut up, okay! So I screwed him! But it's over! Over. We're not sleeping together any more.

STARKEY

You mean you did it more than once?

PATRICIA
(Nods, then looks away)
But it's over.

It suddenly becomes clear to Starkey and he begins to laugh.

STARKEY

You eejit! He's dropped you! You screwed your kidnapper and fell for him and now he's dropped you.

PATRICIA

It's not funny!

STARKEY

Yes, it is! The revenge that caved in on itself. You must feel pretty bloody dirty.

She closes her eyes. He is angry and bitter and wants to say something else . . . but he slowly drops his head and kisses the top of her head. She moves her face up and there are tears in her eyes. He blows a strand of hair away from her face.

PATRICIA

I never kissed him, Dan.

He shakes his head. The strand of hair has fallen down again and he blows it back.

STARKEY
(Softly)

Well, that's okay then.

They look into each other's eyes. We can see that there is still love there.

KEEGAN
(o/s)

Ach, isn't that lovely.

They turn and see him in the doorway. He has a plaster over a split in his nose.

Mad Dog enters the room and advances with a knife in his hand. Patricia instinctively tries to push away as the knife plunges towards her, but she can't go anywhere. Mad Dog cuts the rope that's binding Patricia and Starkey together. He pulls Patricia up and she tries to cling to Starkey, but Mad Dog drags her away. Starkey follows them, passing Keegan in the doorway.

121

INT. APARTMENT – NIGHT

When Starkey and Keegan enter the lounge, Patricia is being held on the ledge by Mad Dog. She looks nervously downwards.

MAD DOG

If you look carefully, you can see Frankie dragging the first pancake away.

As she looks, Mad Dog gives her a shove but holds on to her. She screams and Mad Dog laughs.

Keegan moves across and takes her hand. Mad Dog lets her go and moves behind Starkey. Keegan looks up at Patricia.

STARKEY

There's no need for this.

KEEGAN

Of course there isn't, but it'll speed things up, and it's a good laugh as well . . .

STARKEY

You really are a sick –

KEEGAN

One . . .

STARKEY

Okay! Okay. I don't have the tape, I –

KEEGAN

Two . . .

Listen to me! I had it, I didn't know what was on it. It
was a Dvořák tape for fuck sake. I still don't know. I
needed change for the phone, I sold it to a second-hand
tape stall at the market in Bangor. I swear to God.
(He sighs)
Now let her down.

KEEGAN
Truth?

STARKEY
Truth. Now let her down!

KEEGAN
(Smiles)
Sucker.

Keegan moves to push Patricia over the ledge. She's speechless.
Starkey begins to move towards the window, but they all freeze at
a sudden knocking on the door.

Keegan hesitates, then pulls Patricia in from the window and
pushes her on to a settee. He pushes Starkey there as well. He nods
at Mad Dog, who goes to the door. With the gun in his hand,
Mad Dog opens the door a fraction.

LEE
(o/s)
I'm collecting for the black babies.

MAD DOG
(o/s)

Not now, Sister.

He's closing the door and turning back into the room when the door crashes into him, knocking him flying and the gun out of his hand.

Lee enters the room in full nun regalia, a gun outstretched before her.

LEE

Don't move a fucking muscle!

STARKEY

Lee!

Mad Dog stays where he is while Lee bends and lifts his gun.

LEE
(To Keegan)

Get your fuckin' weapon out and drop it on the fuckin' floor.

She's now brandishing two guns.

Keegan opens his jacket.

KEEGAN

I don't believe in them.

Starkey stands and crosses over to him.

STARKEY

Well, believe in this.

124

He kicks Keegan in the balls and he goes down. Starkey stands over him.

                    PATRICIA
Who the hell is she?

                    STARKEY
Not now, Patricia!

                    PATRICIA
I want to know.

                    LEE
I'm just a friend . . .

                    PATRICIA
As in, what a friend we have in Jesus, or have you been –

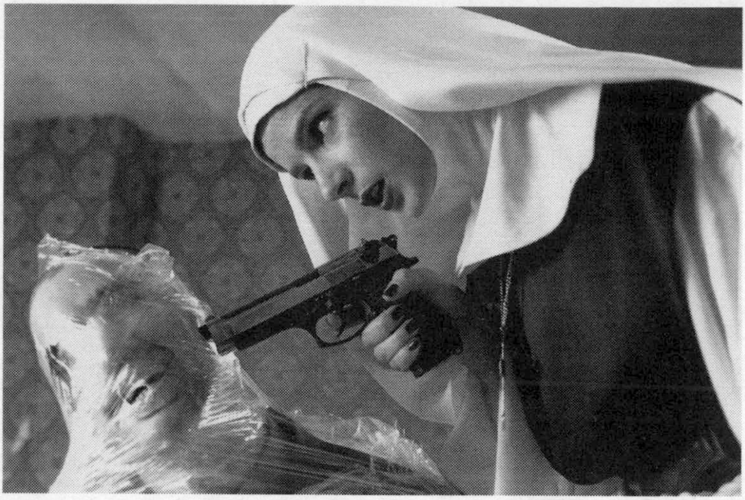

STARKEY

Patricia!

INT. APARTMENT – LATER

Keegan is hanging by a rope outside the apartment. He looks nervously back.

Lee is covering Mad Dog with clingfilm on the floor. She has the guns stuck in the belt of her habit. His whole body is covered in the transparent film, save for his face, which she is just starting.

MAD DOG

Please. Not my –

She clingfilms his face. He sucks the clingfilm in as he gasps for air. She looks at him for a moment, then sticks two fingers up his nostrils, breaking the clingfilm. He yells and she looks horrified.

Starkey has a smile on his face and a knife on the rope holding Keegan in place. He cuts a little into the rope, causing several strands to break.

STARKEY

Not so much fun now, eh?

KEEGAN
(To Patricia)
You're not going to let him do this? Not after what we –

PATRICIA
(Impassively)
I fell for you. Now you fall for me.

STARKEY

So, before you go, about this tape. What's so special?

KEEGAN

I don't know. It's just . . . special.

STARKEY

One . . .

Starkey runs the knife along the rope again and another few strands give way. Keegan drops a couple of feet.

KEEGAN

Jesus! All I know is McGarry was looking a hundred grand for it. That's not the way things work, but everyone was keen for a listen.

STARKEY

Two . . .

KEEGAN

Okay! So there's something about Brinn on it. I don't know what. But that's the game: get the tape, use it to keep him off the throne. McGarry panicked when no one would buy, but instead of destroying it he hid it with Margaret, somewhere he could have easy access to it. He was a greedy fool, and she died because of it.

STARKEY

You mean you killed her for it . . .

KEEGAN

No! Not Margaret. I loved her.

Keegan looks back out into the darkness.

What'll get me out of this?

STARKEY

An ability to fly.

(Beat)

And three . . .

He raises his hand to slash the rope . . .

PATRICIA

Don't!

(He pauses)

Don't, Dan.

STARKEY

After what he did to you?

PATRICIA

It wasn't rape, Dan. And if you do it, it makes you as bad as him. And you're not.

STARKEY

(Looks at her, trying to make his mind up)

Is that some sort of compliment?

She nods and gives a thin smile.

INT. APARTMENT – NIGHT

Mad Dog is clingfilmed on the floor. Keegan hangs by a thread outside the apartment.

Starkey looks down at him.

STARKEY

You still hangin' around?

KEEGAN

Starkey, I swear to God I –

Starkey laughs and closes the window. As he crosses the room he steps on Mad Dog.

STARKEY

Sorry, didn't see you there.

He follows Lee and Patricia out.

INT. ELEVATOR – NIGHT

Starkey, Lee and Patricia are in the elevator. Lee is brandishing the guns. She looks pleased with herself.

LEE

I haven't had so much fun in years.

INT. APARTMENT BLOCK – NIGHT

The elevator doors open and Starkey, Lee and Patricia exit.

STARKEY

Where'd you get the gun?

EXT. APARTMENT BLOCK – NIGHT

The trio exit the apartment block in single file. They make for an odd sight: the guy with the bruises, the nun with the gun and the dishevelled woman in the pink dressing gown and slippers.

As they come out of the apartment block we see Frankie waiting in the shadows. He clearly hears her reply.

LEE

Replica. I do a stripping policewoman as well. I saw those guys follow you into the restaurant . . . I knew I had to do something.

STARKEY

Well, thank God you did.

PATRICIA

So how did you two . . . ?

STARKEY

Please, Trish, not now . . .

Frankie steps out of the shadows behind them.

FRANKIE

Hold your horses.

They freeze, then turn. Frankie is holding a gun on them.

FRANKIE

I don't know how the fuck yees did it, but I think we better go back inside.

Lee slowly raises a gun and points it at him.

LEE

Mine's bigger than yours.

FRANKIE

Aye. Go on. Shoot me.

131

She shoots him.

He looks extremely surprised. There's a bullet hole in the middle of his forehead.

LEE

Holy Mother of God!

She looks at the gun, then drops it. Frankie slowly folds to the ground. Lee removes her replica pistol from her belt and studies it, mesmerised.

Patricia grabs Lee's arm and hurries her along as Lee looks back at the body.

INT. HOUSE – DAY

We're in a suburban bedroom and a phone is ringing. Mouse's head appears from beneath the blankets and he reaches for the phone.

MOUSE

WHAT?

STARKEY
(o/s)

That's not a very pleasant greeting, Mouse.

MOUSE

Dan?

STARKEY

Y'know, Mouse, if the line is bugged, speaking quieter isn't going to fool them.

132

MOUSE

Of course the line isn't bugged, Danny Boy.

EXT. STREET – DAY

Starkey is in a phone box. The Mini, with Patricia and Lee
waiting with the engine running, is in the background.

Starkey realises there's something not right about Mouse's
response. He pauses, looks mildly panicked, then speaks rapidly.

STARKEY

I need a car. See you at the monkey puzzle tree in
twenty minutes.

He slams the phone down, then steps back from it, like it could
shop him. He climbs back into the car and slams the door. As the
car sets off we hear:

LEE
(o/s)

Where's the monkey puzzle tree?

STARKEY
(o/s)

There is no monkey puzzle tree.

EXT. PARK – DAY

It is the park where Starkey first met Margaret. It has turned into
a beautiful morning.

Mouse walks nervously along a path, skirting the grass.

133

STARKEY
(v/o)

We drank here as kids. Back when we had no worries.
Or when our only worries where about getting served,
about getting a girl. When murder was a hangover.

*Mouse stops and pretends to tie his shoe. He's so busy looking in
one direction that when he stands up he almost collides with a
troop of Brownies marching past. He lets out a little shout and
jumps back. The Brownie leader gives him a filthy look and
marches on.*

STARKEY
(v/o)

We always called it the monkey puzzle tree, 'cause
Mouse told us that's what it was. But it wasn't. And he
knew better than to call me Danny Boy.

*When Mouse turns again, Starkey has emerged from the bushes at
the base of a large tree. He stands with his arms folded, looking at
Mouse. Mouse looks back.*

MOUSE

I told you not to mess with the wee dolls.

STARKEY

Were you able to get a car?

MOUSE

I hired one. It's an automatic and takes unleaded petrol.
There's half a tank in it and three vouchers towards a
plastic beaker with George Best's head on it.
(Beat)
Do you want to tell me what's going on?

134

STARKEY

No.

MOUSE

Or where you're going?

STARKEY

No.

He's embarrassed and looks at his shoes.

MOUSE

Dan, you didn't do everything they say, did you?

Starkey just looks at him. Mouse sighs.

What about Patricia?

STARKEY
            (As Patricia emerges from the bushes)
That Patricia?

MOUSE

Jesus, Patricia, I thought . . .

Then Lee emerges, the nun with the gun.

Oh my God.

STARKEY

I need you to look after them, Mouse. Can you do that?
Just until I get things sorted out.

MOUSE

Of course . . . I just . . .

Starkey strides forward and takes the car keys off Mouse.

Thanks, Mouse.

MOUSE

It's what friends are for, mate.

Starkey turns to Patricia and looks awkwardly at her.

PATRICIA

You don't have to do this.

STARKEY

Aye, I know. But someone does, and it may as well be one of the good guys.

PATRICIA
(She smiles)

You are a good guy.

136

                    STARKEY

I have my moments.

He gives her a shy smile, then a quick kiss.

                    STARKEY

Those lips are my lips. I'll be back for them.

He pulls on his wig again.

Patricia puts her fingers to her lips and watches him go. Lee comes to stand by her side, watching him also. Mouse puts a hand on Patricia's shoulder.

                    MOUSE

He'll be back.
                    (She nods slowly)
I didn't tell him which car it was.

EXT. MARKET – DAY

Starkey is rifling through one of the boxes of tapes. The Sod stands back, watching him. He's chewing a matchstick.

                    SOD

Collector's item, was it?

                    STARKEY

It's worth nothing. My ma's, sentimental value.

The Sod nods and rubs a finger over his lip.

                    SOD

I think . . . was it the one with all the Vikings and stuff on the front?
                    (Starkey nods)

                    137

Aye, aye. Now what happened to it . . . I just can't . . .

Starkey sighs, fishes a tenner out and offers it across.

STARKEY

Maybe this will help . . .

SOD

Aye, it's coming back, but it's just not quite there . . .

Starkey grabs him and bangs his head down on the table.

STARKEY

I need the fucking tape. Now either you tell me or you
get the collected works of Englebert Humperdink up
your fucking arse.

*He releases the Sod, who looks up, the matchstick broken in his
mouth and attached to his upper lip.*

SOD

Okay . . . okay! Jesus . . . okay. A priest . . . y'know . . .
gave me a few quid for it . . .

STARKEY

Did you get his name? Did he write you a cheque?

SOD

No, I don't know . . . He was just passing through. Said
he was from Crossmaheart.

Starkey lets the Sod go and stands back.

STARKEY

Crossmaheart.

SOD
(Brushing himself down)

Aye. In the heart of the Congo.

Starkey takes another tenner and hands it across. He raises his eyebrows apologetically then turns away, but as he does he spots Mad Dog and several cronies looking about the market for the stall.

Starkey turns back and dives beneath the canvas stall cover.

SOD

Hey, c'mon now . . .

We see a hand coming out with three tenners in it.

STARKEY

Just shut the fuck up.

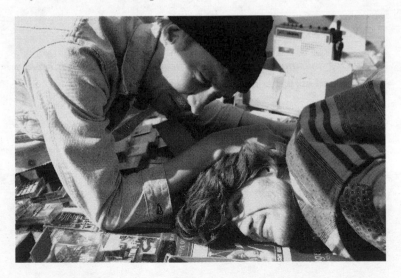

The Sod crumples the tenners into his pocket and looks up to see
Mad Dog and his cronies approaching. Mad Dog runs his finger
down the line of tapes. The Sod nervously sticks another match in
his mouth.

                          MAD DOG
I'm looking for Divor-ak.

                            SOD
Divor-ak hasn't been in today yet.

The Sod's head hits the table for the second time.

                          MAD DOG
I'm looking for a tape of Divor-ak.

                            SOD
                         (In pain)
We have quite a few. He's hardly Mr Popular.

Mad Dog pulls the Sod up again. The second matchstick is broken
and stuck to his upper lip.

                          MAD DOG
Give me them. Now.

The Sod hurriedly sorts through his tapes, picking out five in
rapid succession.

                            SOD
Five quid.

MAD DOG
(Snorts)

Aye.

*He takes the tapes and turns away. The cronies give the Sod a
dirty look, then go after Mad Dog.*

CRONY 1

What does Divor-ak sing anyway?

As they disappear, Starkey comes out from beneath the stall.

SOD

What the fuck was that about?

STARKEY

I told you, it has sentimental value.

EXT. CROSSMAHEART – DAY

*Starkey stops the car at the top of a hill which affords him a view
over the murky-looking town of Crossmaheart. A military
helicopter clatters overhead. We focus in on a chapel on the edge of
town.*

*Starkey drives through the town of Crossmaheart. Shops are
shuttered, houses bricked up, the burnt-out remains of cars litter
the roads which are covered in glass. Scruffy kids hang out on
street corners, others bang hurly sticks against kerbs. Irish
Republic flags flutter from telegraph poles.*

STARKEY
(v/o)

In the early seventies, when religious riots were tearing
Belfast apart, someone had the bright idea of shipping

whole communities out of the city, giving them new houses and state-supported industry. It would be Shangri-o-la. Except you don't treat bubonic plague by moving the victims to uninfected areas. Crossmaheart was soon as wild and wicked as anything in Belfast, and one man cracked the whip: Cow Pat Keegan.

EXT. CHAPEL – DAY

Starkey gets out of the car and enters the grounds of a chapel with its attendant graveyard and priest's house. Father Flynn is jabbing rubbish in the graveyard with a pointed stick, carrying a black bin bag in his other hand. It seems quite full. He lifts the stick up in the air and examines something caught on the end of it: a used condom. His face crinkles up in disgust.

STARKEY

Father Flynn?

Flynn raises an eyebrow, and for a few moments they both study the condom.

FLYNN

Of course, we have recently given some ground on the subject of contraception, but I don't think His Holiness specifically meant the church grounds.
  (He laughs and puts the condom in the bin bag)
Now, son, what can I be doing you for?

STARKEY

I'm sorry to disturb you, it's –

FLYNN

Is it a confession? You're getting married? A vexing point of theology?

142

STARKEY

No, Father, it's not a religious problem, I . . .

FLYNN
(He stops and sighs)

Oh, I might have known. You may proceed directly to
the abuse then. Go on. Hit me with it. Though I doubt
you'll come up with anything new. I believe Antichrist
was the last one.

STARKEY

Are the Protestants giving you a hard time, Father?

FLYNN

Protestants? Not a bit of it, they're fine! You mean
you're not . . . ?
(He brightens considerably)
Come on inside with me, lad, I want to show you my
chest . . .

*He signals for Starkey to follow him and walks towards the
chapel. Starkey follows warily, looking about him as if he is being
led into a trap.*

INT. CHAPEL – DAY

*Father Flynn stands at the top of the chapel. He removes his dog
collar, then begins to unbutton his shirt. Starkey stands a little
back from him, not sure where to look. He looks up at Christ on
the cross. When he looks back at Flynn he is naked from the waist
up, and has spread his arms in an unintentionally Christ-like
pose.*

144

FLYNN

Well, what do you think?

STARKEY

Father, I'm not here to . . .

FLYNN

Be there for life, of course, but at least there is a life.

He runs a finger down his chest; Starkey looks closer.

STARKEY

Jes . . . They stabbed you?

FLYNN

No! Well, in a way . . . Heart transplant!
        (He bangs his chest)
Sound as a pound now, but they'd booked the coffin and
all . . . Then I came home, bright as a button.

STARKEY

So what's the problem?

FLYNN

The story got out that the English had played a trick on
me. That they'd given me a Protestant's heart. And there
hasn't been a sinner through those doors since!

*He laughs, claps his hands together, then lifts his shirt and begins
to dress.*

STARKEY

Father, I'm here about a cassette tape you bought in
Bangor the other day.

145

FLYNN

A tape? Y'mean yon cheap thing I picked up in the market?

STARKEY

Yes, Father, I'm afraid it was sold to you by mistake, it was my mother's and –

FLYNN

Oh dear, now . . . your mother's? Oh dear. She knows Michael Brinn, does she?

STARKEY

You've listened to it?

FLYNN

Of course I have. Even as they're counting the votes, I'd say our Mr Brinn had problems.

INT. CHURCH – LATER

We hear a man sobbing. We see Gospel scenes on the stained-glass windows. We see Christ on the cross. We see the tape turning round in a tape machine attached to the church PA system.

Starkey sits in a pew, head in hands; Father Flynn sits beside him, eyes closed.

STARKEY

I thought it was another woman. That he'd been careless with a phone call. Or another man.

146

BRINN

On tape, still sobbing, which echoes eerily around the church.

I thought I was doing the right thing, doing my bit for Ireland. But they knew it was double booked, they just didn't tell me . . .

FLYNN

He was planting the bomb in the Conway Hotel when it went off prematurely. He was in the IRA. He killed thirteen people in that blast.

STARKEY

Fuck.

FLYNN

Fuck indeed.

EXT. CROSSMAHEART – DAY

Starkey is driving back towards the town. We still hear the tape playing . . .

BRINN
(o/s, sobbing)
Burnt alive, just ordinary people, kids . . .

McGARRY
(o/s)
You couldn't have known . . .

BRINN
(o/s)
I should have known . . . Oh, God, I wish I'd died . . .

EXT. CROSSMAHEART – DAY

Starkey parks his car on Crossmaheart's main street and ejects the tape. He gets out of the car and walks across the pavement to the post office.

INT. POST OFFICE – DAY

The post office door opens and Starkey enters. A young man sitting behind a heavily-fortified counter looks up. He is reading a book: Dr Zhivago.

Starkey approaches the counter and lifts down a small padded envelope from a display. As he talks, he begins to write an address on the envelope.

> POSTAL
>
> Howdy.

> STARKEY
>
> All right. Quiet in here.

Starkey moves the envelope below the counter so that Postal can't see it, then slips the cassette into it and seals it.

> POSTAL
>
> Only busy on giro day. Then it's pandemonium. So what can I do for you?

> STARKEY
>
> Can you send this first class?

> POSTAL
>
> I'm afraid we only do second class, to reflect the standard of our clientele.

STARKEY

That's a damning indictment of your clientele.

POSTAL

You haven't met them yet.

STARKEY

You must make a lot of friends with that attitude.

POSTAL

On the contrary.

Starkey tries to squeeze the envelope under the security grille.
Postal helps to pull it through, then looks at the address. He shakes
the envelope.

POSTAL

Anything valuable?

STARKEY

No.

POSTAL

Are you sure? Do you want it recorded delivery?
Registered? Guaranteed next day –

STARKEY
(Barks)

Could you just post it?

Sees the disappointment on Postal's face and sighs.

Okay, guaranteed. Next day.

POSTAL

Guaranteed! Next day! Absolutely! That's £3.20.

Starkey counts out some change.

Do you want a receipt?

STARKEY

No.

POSTAL

Are you sure?

(Starkey shakes his head)

Suit yourself.

Starkey turns away from the counter and goes to the door. He opens it, then stops.

STARKEY

Dr Zhivago?

POSTAL

(Lifting the book)

Yeah. It's great.

STARKEY

See the movie?

POSTAL

Nah, I prefer –

STARKEY

You know he dies in the end?

Starkey exits.

EXT. CROSSMAHEART – DAY

As Starkey approaches the car he sees that Mad Dog is sitting on the bonnet. He stops, thinks about fleeing, then realises that two other thugs have appeared behind him.

> MAD DOG
>
> They seek him here, they seek him there. Get in the fuckin' car, y'arsehole.

> STARKEY
>
> Do you want me to drive?

> MAD DOG
>
> Gimme the keys.

> STARKEY
>
> But you're not insured.

> MAD DOG
>
> Gimme the fuckin' keys, Starkey.

Starkey gives him the keys. One of the hoods guides him into the back seat. A gun is immediately placed against his head. The other hood searches him.

> MAD DOG
>
> Where's the tape?

> STARKEY
>
> What tape?

One of the hoods cracks the gun off Starkey's skull; he starts to bleed. When he looks up he sees that a large, red, heavy

*armour-plated Post Office van (possibly an adapted Army Pig)
has arrived at the post office, and mail is being loaded aboard.*

MAD DOG

What's the point in this? You're only going to end up
brain damaged.

Starkey nods as he sees the Post Office van close up.

STARKEY

What's it like?

The hood goes to hit him again, but Mad Dog catches his arm.

MAD DOG

Save it.

*The car starts and pulls out into the traffic. The Post Office van
follows behind.*

MAD DOG

You're your own worst enemy, Starkey.

STARKEY

Aye, ah know.
                        (Beat)
You know that tape's worth a fortune?

Mad Dog looks round at him.

MAD DOG

Don't even suggest it, son.

As they come to a junction, the Post Office van turns off.

EXT. CROSSMAHEART – DAY

The car arrives at a large, run-down housing estate. The houses are uniformly similar: all in need of repair, their gardens overgrown. The street is strewn with glass and burnt-out cars; kids and men hang about, looking bored. It's the Congo.

The car pulls up outside a long terrace. The houses are all in poor condition except for the one at the gable end which has stone cladding, a satellite dish, security cameras, a Porsche out front, a pond in the front garden, a bird table and garden gnomes (three normal, one with a balaclava on and holding a kalashnikov instead of a fishing rod).

> STARKEY
>
> Which one's Cow Pat's?

INT. KEEGAN'S HOUSE – DAY

Starkey sits looking defeated in the front room of Keegan's house. Keegan, master of his own and anybody else's domain, circles around him. There is a large painting of Margaret on the wall.

> KEEGAN
>
> It's funny what attracts two people, isn't it?

> STARKEY
>
> I'm sorry?

> KEEGAN
>
> Sexual chemistry. I mean, me and Margaret, you and Margaret, me and your wife, you and your wife. I suppose to complete the circle you should really sleep with my wife. Although I wouldn't recommend it.

STARKEY

Crap, is she?

KEEGAN
(Ignoring him)

You listened to the tape?

STARKEY

Aye. He confesses to the –

KEEGAN

Bombing of the Conway Hotel, yes, I know. So you can appreciate how desperate he is to get it back. And how keen I am to get hold of it.

STARKEY

I don't have it.

KEEGAN

Let's not go down this road again, Starkey.

STARKEY

I don't have it . . .

KEEGAN

You know exactly where it is. So here's what I want you to do: you go and see Michael Brinn. You tell him I want to deal. Tell him to bring £1,000,000 to the Silent Valley tomorrow at dawn. Him, and him alone. I want you to join us as well. Bring the tape with you. Then we'll all have a little powwow.

154

STARKEY

And why the fuck would I want to go along with all that?

KEEGAN

Because otherwise Mad Dog is going to torture you to
within an inch of your life. And then I'll come in and
take the other fucking inch personally.

STARKEY
(Thinking for a moment)
Nah, it's all right. I'll go for the torture.

KEEGAN
(Surprised)
What're you protecting him for?

STARKEY

I'm not protecting him. I know what he's done and it'll
catch up with him one day. But if it comes down to who
I'd rather have running the country, I'll choose him over
you every fucking time.

KEEGAN

Would you really now? I wonder . . . I'll tell you what,
my newly-principled little friend. Let's make it easier for
you.
(He looks at his watch)
As of thirty minutes ago your – and my – lovely Patricia,
the nun and a man who appears to go by the name of
Mouse are being held under my protection in Belfast.
(Beat)
You're not as smart as you think.

155

STARKEY
I never claimed to be smart.

EXT. KEEGAN'S HOUSE – DAY

Starkey is sitting in his car. The hoods are loosely grouped about it.

STARKEY
. . . what if I'm stopped, what if someone recognises –

KEEGAN
You'll get through. It's arranged.

Starkey gives him a look, then drives slowly forward. Keegan turns back into the house.

Starkey stops the car and reverses back. His head juts out the window.

STARKEY
I don't even know his number if something goes wrong.

One of the hoods kneels beside the car.

HOOD
It's in the book. Under K. For kunt.

EXT. COUNTRY ROAD – DAY

Starkey drives, looking nervously about him. He passes a telephone box, slows down, then reverses back. He jumps out and dials a number.

                    VOICE
                    (o/s)
Hello?

                    STARKEY
Mouse?

                    HOOD
                    (o/s)
Starkey, if that's you, just stop pissin' around and get the
job done.

*Starkey slams the phone down and hurries back to the car. As the
car continues on its way we hear the radio:*

                    ANNOUNCER
                    (o/s)
. . . have estimated an 80% turnout, the highest on
record. Counting will continue through the night, with
the first results expected at around 4 a.m. A BBC exit
poll suggests that Michael Brinn is commanding the
overwhelming –

*A button is pushed, and we hear the sounds of country and
western.*

                    STARKEY
                    (Softly)
Fuckin' Jim Reeves.

EXT. ROAD – DAY

*Starkey rounds a corner and sees that the road immediately ahead
is blocked. Two guys in white shirts, ties and shoulder holsters
lean nonchalantly against a car, chewing gum. Starkey brakes*

                    157

and throws the car into reverse, but another car comes up from behind and blocks his escape.

One of the gum chewers pushes himself off the car and opens the back door. Alfie Stewart steps out. Another opens Starkey's door.

> GUY

Step out of the car.

Starkey climbs out of the vehicle.

> ALFIE

Dan, your own personal escort service. In the back.

Starkey doesn't say anything. He crosses to the car and opens the back door, but Stewart slams it shut.

> ALFIE

When I say the back, I mean the back.

He lifts the boot, then nods for Starkey to get in. Starkey hesitates again, then climbs in. We see from his POV the boot slamming down.

EXT. RED HALL – DAY

The heavily-armed gates at Red Hall swing open and the Jag sweeps into the driveway, up towards the building, then disappears round the back.

EXT. RED HALL – DAY

Starkey enters an enclosed courtyard which is bathed in sunlight. He stands awkwardly for a moment, then is surprised by a voice.

AGNES

Come on down, the party's just beginning.

Starkey sees the back of a sun lounger and the top of Agnes's head; she is holding up a drink. He walks forward.

STARKEY

I thought you'd be out with him at the polls. Basking in the glory . . .

She is wearing a swimsuit and sunglasses. She smiles. She's quite obviously pregnant.

Oh . . .

She sees the look of surprise on his face and puts her hand on the bump.

AGNES

We were holding it in reserve in case the exit polls had us really close. Alfie reckoned it was worth a couple of thousand votes.

She strokes her stomach and looks at Starkey. Sadly.

The future's bright, the future's Brinn.

STARKEY

Are you okay?

AGNES

Oh, I'm fine. What about you?

STARKEY

I'm young, I have my health, I'm public enemy number one.

AGNES

You didn't really kill her, did you?

STARKEY

No.

AGNES

He didn't think you did. But you were having an affair
with her.

STARKEY

I was.

AGNES

An affair.

(She sighs)

You love your wife?

STARKEY

I do.

AGNES

But how could you if you wanted to go off and have sex
with someone else?

STARKEY

Maybe love isn't as clear cut as that. Has your dear
husband ever been unfaithful?

AGNES

No. Of course not.

160

STARKEY

Mr Charming himself, who has half the women in Ulster eating out of his pants?

AGNES

I would know.

STARKEY

Like you knew about the bomb?

She looks away. Tears begin to roll down her cheeks.

AGNES

It's all going to end, isn't it, before it's even begun?

STARKEY

I don't know. I really don't know.

She puts her hand out to him. He grasps it.

STARKEY

It's not you.

AGNES

No, it's not. But it might as well be.

INT. RED HALL – DAY

Brinn stands by the study window, looking down at his wife drinking in the courtyard. Starkey stands behind him.

BRINN

One million for Cow Pat Keegan on a lonely road at dawn. He has a great sense of drama.

161

STARKEY

Are you going to pay him?

BRINN

Yes, I'm going to pay him.

STARKEY

You think that'll be the end of it?

BRINN
(Beat)

She hasn't taken it well.

STARKEY

It must have come as a shock.

Brinn turns from the window.

BRINN

It came as a shock to me. Now you know why I don't
touch alcohol. One drunken night with David McGarry.
He was my best friend. Or I thought he was.
(Laughs)
Male bonding. We told each other everything, but he was
recording it. And now here you are, the devil's advocate.

STARKEY

That's a drink made with eggs, isn't it? No wonder he's
so evil, it tastes like shite.

BRINN

Oh, what a performer, laughing in the face of death.

STARKEY

Well, you would know more about death than me.

BRINN

Yes. Indeed.
                    (Beat)
When you're young, you're so certain about things.
There's no grey, there's just black and white. I had this
burning fervour for Ireland.

He examines the burns on his lower arm. Sighs and says
non-flippantly:

Then I just had the burning.

STARKEY

Have you ever come across words like guilt, or remorse?

Brinn looks at him, steely now, with less of the oiliness . . .

All of this is about guilt, it's all about remorse. I made
my mistake. I'm making amends. I can make things right,
I just need the chance.

They stare at each other. Beat.

He doesn't have the tape, does he? If he had it, he wouldn't
bother sending you here. He'd deal direct.
(Beat)
It's you. You have it.
(Starkey shrugs)
So what's he offered you, Dan? Money is it? Or is this
just another exclusive?

STARKEY

He's holding my wife.

BRINN
(Nodding slowly)
Okay. Sorry.

STARKEY

I lost her once, I don't want to lose her again.

BRINN

If he gets hold of that tape, Dan, there will be anarchy.
Ten thousand people will die. I guarantee it. Will you
accept that responsibility? One life against ten thousand.

STARKEY
(Nods at the window)
Would you let your wife die, if it meant peace?

164

BRINN
(Nods slowly again)
Sometimes you have to look beyond the individual.

Starkey shakes his head, then turns and exits as Brinn stares after him.

EXT. BELFAST STREET – NIGHT

A dark and scary alley in downtown Belfast. A car boot slams and Alfie Stewart's Jag roars away into the night. Starkey pulls his collar up, slips his hand into his pocket and starts to walk.

EXT. MARGARET'S HOUSE – NIGHT

Starkey stands in the shadows opposite Margaret's boarded-up house as two drunks make their way past it. When they've gone, he hurries across the road and begins to pry the boards away, trying to make himself small as a car passes.

INT. MARGARET'S HOUSE – DAWN

Starkey is curled up before the front door. He is woken by a package coming through the letter box. When he stands to open it, we see the chalk outline of Margaret's mother's body on the floor.

EXT. RED HALL – DAWN

Alfie Stewart is in the car park at Red Hall, leaning against a car with the engine running. The hall is decorated with bunting and balloons: victory.

Michael Brinn is in the doorway, saying good-bye to his wife. He goes to kiss her but she turns her cheek. He walks across to the car. Stewart opens the door for him, then goes round to the other side.

*As Brinn climbs in the driver turns to him and nods. It is Billy
McCoubrey. He hands a briefcase back to Brinn, who nods.
Silently, they set off.*

EXT. KEEGAN'S HOUSE – DAWN

*There is a Land Rover with engine running and hoods lolling
against it outside the house. They are all carrying guns. The front
door opens and Keegan emerges, carrying a kalashnikov.*

KEEGAN

We ride, *muchachos.*

EXT. ROAD – DAWN

*McCoubrey drives through the town. He passes cars pumping
their horns, people waving the UN Peace Flag, revellers drunk but
happy . . .*

RADIO
(v/o)

. . . will assume power later today and then announce
details of his first cabinet at a press conference to be held
in –

*McCoubrey turns the radio off. He glances at the briefcase lying
on the seat beside him.*

EXT. ROAD – DAWN

*Keegan's Land Rover is slowly cruising towards the meeting with
Brinn. It comes to a halt on a misty road flanked by dark,
looming pines. Keegan and his crew get out of the Land Rover,
and begin to check their weapons. Brinn's car comes to a halt*

about twenty yards away. Alfie Stewart gets out, opens Brinn's door. Then McCoubrey climbs out. For several moments the two parties stare at each other without moving.

Then we hear the sound of a diesel engine and a taxi comes to a halt. When it moves on we see Starkey standing equidistant from the two sides. He looks left and right, then Keegan and his men begin to move forward. Brinn's group then follows until they all meet up in the middle. Starkey's looking oddly at McCoubrey, trying to work out his role.

STARKEY

Michael Brinn, Cow Pat –

BRINN

Hello, Pat. Long time.

STARKEY

You know . . . ?

KEEGAN

We share an interest in hotels. Police dinners our speciality.

BRINN

Except you knew they'd pulled out.

KEEGAN

Ah, now, but a bomb's a bomb. Besides, look what an illustrious career I kick-started. I thought I specified that you come alone.

167

BRINN

I'm not as naive as I used to be. A little immoral support.
You have the tape?

KEEGAN

You have the money?

*Keegan looks to Starkey, who produces the tape and hands it to
Keegan who then hands the tape back over his shoulder to one of
his hoods.*

BRINN

You always loved your little games.

KEEGAN

I thought it was a nice touch of irony. You have
Margaret killed, her lover brings you salvation.

STARKEY

You . . .

I didn't. The dream team here overstepped the mark.
Her father betrayed us, everything was in the balance . . .
it just got out of hand.

*Realisation dawns on Starkey; he glares at McCoubrey, who
looks smug and winks at him.*

I'm sorry.

He sighs. He should leave it at that.

But we're back to individuals again, Dan . . .

*Starkey looks from one to the other, horrified. For the first time he
really begins to crumble.*

STARKEY

Individuals? It's individuals went out of their fucking way
to vote for you. Individuals giving up their fucking
heritage to put you in power. Indi-fucking-viduals. I'm
an individual. You're an individual. Dougal from the
fucking Magic Roundabout is an individual. And you're
both the fucking same, we're going straight back to civil
war here because you don't give a fuck about –

KEEGAN

Individuals. We get the point. Now shut the fuck –

Starkey pulls away from Mad Dog's restraining arm.

STARKEY

No! No. Make me. You're gonna bloody kill me anyway.
The problem with you two, it's all numbers. One million

169

pounds, ten thousand dead, thirteen skeletons . . .
numbers.

(He clicks his fingers)

And it's easy, because numbers aren't people. Numbers
don't think for themselves. They don't go out for a pint
with the lads, they don't throw potatoes through windows
and they don't kiss you the best fucking kiss in the world
goodnight. Do you understand?

BRINN

Scratch a dipso journalist, there's a little philosopher
waiting to come out.

STARKEY

Fuck you, Prime Minister.

*He punches him and Brinn reels back. Mad Dog cracks Starkey
with a gun and he crashes to the ground. McCoubrey comes
menacingly forward, about to hammer Starkey, but Brinn holds
him back.*

Brinn, patting his cheek, stands over Starkey.

BRINN

See what I mean about peace? It's easier said than
practised.

(To Keegan)

This is a one-off payment for your silence. Try it again
and I'll break you.

*Keegan turns to a hood, nods, and is handed a portable cassette
player which he hands to Brinn.*

KEEGAN

You can't say we're not good to you, Michael: something

to play it on as well. But let's have a wee listen now, make sure it's authentic.

Keegan presses the play button and we see the tape go round. We hear a snatch of the tape. Keegan smiles, stops the tape and hands it to Brinn. Alfie Stewart hands the case with the money to Keegan's man.

Brinn and Keegan look at each other. Brinn nods, then turns towards the car, his henchmen go with him. Then he stops.

BRINN

Do you want me to take the reporter with me?

Keegan looks at Starkey, then at Mad Dog. Then he shakes his head; there's the hint of a smile.

KEEGAN

I think we'll hold on to him for a little while.

Brinn nods, climbs into his car and drives off. The hoods gather in the road, looking after him.

INT. CAR – DAWN

Brinn's in the back seat of the car. They've all got serious faces. Then Brinn starts to laugh. The others join in. He removes the cassette player from his coat and sets it on his lap. He presses the eject button.

EXT. COUNTRY ROAD – DAWN

Brinn's car explodes in a ball of flame. Far back up the road the hoods surrounding Keegan burst into applause.

KEEGAN

I thought you said those were long-life batteries.

The hoods laugh.

Starkey is mesmerised by the explosion.

KEEGAN

Bet you're glad you stayed behind now.
                    (Beat)
Oh, don't look so shocked.

Mad Dog cocks the gun at Starkey's head.

MAD DOG

Boss?

Keegan hesitates. Starkey, a bloody mess already, is helpless.
Then Keegan walks across and boots Starkey in the balls. Starkey
hits the ground, groaning.

KEEGAN

Just returning the compliment, Dan.
                    (Beat)
But, no. I think we'll leave him.

He kneels down beside Starkey.

You're alive because if you loved Margaret half as much as
I did, then you'll want to write about her, about who killed
her. People should know she wasn't a martyr to peace.

Keegan stands, then leads his men back down the road towards
their Land Rover. Starkey raises himself painfully to his knees. At

173

one end of the road we see the smoking remains of Brinn's car, at the other end Keegan's Land Rover setting off.

INT. LAND ROVER – DAY

The mood in the Land Rover is upbeat. Keegan is in the passenger seat, briefcase on his lap. He puts his fingers on the lock, about to open it.

> KEEGAN
> You'll be thinking this round's on me.

We focus for a second on the lock. He pushes it, we pause, waiting for something to happen, but nothing happens. Keegan opens the case and looks at the money sitting in neat elastic-banded piles. He lifts one of the piles.

EXT. ROAD – DAY

As Starkey looks at the Land Rover, Mad Dog leans out the back and gives him two fingers. As he does, the vehicle explodes with considerable force. Starkey is thrown to the ground. He crawls, gets to his hands and knees and finally begins to stagger away, but he's between two burning wrecks. He comes to a stop. He can't run any more. He's at the end of his tether. He sinks to the ground. Then he sits there. He pulls up his collar. He waits. His vision begins to fade. We hear the beat of helicopters.

INT. HOSPITAL ROOM – DAY

Starkey's in bed in a private hospital room, his head bandaged. His eyes are closed, but he's beginning to come round. We see Lee, in her nurse's uniform, looking down at him; she looks concerned, but a smile starts to move across her face as he regains consciousness.

STARKEY
(Groggily)

Patricia?

The smile fades, replaced by a look of sad resignation.

LEE

She's okay. We're all okay. They let us go.

Starkey tries to get up out of the bed.

STARKEY

But the police . . . I have to . . . my shoes . . .

She calms him down.

LEE

It's okay. Everything's fine . . . They know about it all.
Just take it easy.

*Starkey falls back on his pillow, closes his eyes, then opens them
again and looks at her.*

STARKEY

They're all dead?

LEE
(She nods)

It's chaos out there. But then it always has been.

*There's movement at the door. Starkey looks up to see two senior
police officers and an imposing-looking civil servant.*

175

LEE

They've been waiting. I have to go . . . More shite to
shovel.

She smiles sadly at him then leaves the room as the men enter.

INT. HOSPITAL – DAY

*Starkey, fully dressed now, is marching down the hospital corridor
with the police, a gaggle of civil servants and a very
hassled-looking figure of authority in pursuit. Starkey pushes
through some swing doors.*

SECRETARY OF STATE

We're not saying you can't write about it, we'd just
prefer if you didn't . . .

STARKEY

I'm sure you would.

SECRETARY OF STATE

You've got to think of the stability of the country, the
harm this could . . .

Starkey stops suddenly and pokes the Secretary of State.

STARKEY

Am I wanted for any crime, Mister Secretary of State?

SECRETARY OF STATE

Not now, no.

STARKEY

Right, you can fuck off then.

176

SECRETARY OF STATE

Her Majesty has asked me to personally urge you not to write –

STARKEY
(Stopping suddenly)

Is she going to make me the Duke of Westminster? Or the Count of Monte Cristo?

SECRETARY OF STATE

No.

STARKEY

Right, well she can fuck off as well then.

He pushes through the hospital doors into bright sunlight.

EXT. HOSPITAL – DAY

Starkey emerges from the hospital. He looks to his right. There is a horde of press and TV people loitering by a fence, chatting, bored. Someone notices him, points, and they begin to run towards him.

Starkey dives into the back of a taxi, which roars off. We see a hand coming out of the driver's window, two fingers waved back at the reporters and a shout of

> DRIVER
>
> Fuck yees!

Starkey watches the reporters for a moment, then turns back to the driver. She's the driver from before, grinning back at him.

> DRIVER
>
> Hey, how the fuck are ye?
> *(Beat)*
> Yer gob's been all over the box. The husband says to me, you should call the fuckin' peelers, tell them he was in your taxi. Says I, Billy, will you shut the fuck up.

> STARKEY
>
> Thanks.

The taxi drives through the centre of Belfast. Starkey is in the back, staring listlessly at the shops. There are troops on the streets, burnt-out cars, the Union Flag is flying again, kids are re-painting the paramilitary murals . . .

> STARKEY
> *(v/o)*
> I don't know what I'll write. Maybe about love and betrayal, war and peace. Maybe about Parker and

learning to fly. Or about Margaret and how a single
stolen moment can change the fate of a . . .
(Sighs)
I just hope it'll be better than the other shite.

EXT. STARKEY'S HOUSE – DAY

*Starkey gets out of the taxi, bends back in with a fiver. The driver
snaps the money off him.*

STARKEY

Sorry I've nothing extra for –

DRIVER

Big fuckin' head, tight fuckin' arse.

*He closes the door and turns to the house. The taxi roars off; horns
sound behind him as the driver narrowly avoids a collision; we
hear her yelling at someone.*

*Starkey stops by the front door. He looks up and down the street,
then takes a deep breath and reaches up to knock on the door.
Before he can, the door opens. Patricia stands there, looking rather
wonderful.*

PATRICIA

I heard the taxi.

*He nods. She stands aside and he enters the house. She closes the
door.*

INT. HOUSE – DAY

*Starkey and Patricia sit apart on the Magic Settee. They both
look ahead, awkwardly.*

So, how's married life treating you?

Beat. She ignores this.

Guy that owns this house says this is a magic settee. Every time you . . .

They look at each other. Then the picture freezes just as they begin to collapse into each other's arms. We hear 'Good Year for the Roses' by Elvis Costello, or a similar sad country classic.

BBC Films, Winchester Films and Scala present in association with The Arts
Council of England and The Arts Council of Northern Ireland a Scala Production
in association with IMA Films and Le Studio Canal+

DAVID THEWLIS
RACHEL GRIFFITHS
JASON ISAACS

DIVORCING JACK

LAURA FRASER
RICHARD GANT
LAINE MEGAW
BRONAGH GALLAGHER
KITTY ALDRIDGE
ROBERT LINDSAY

Casting
ROS & JOHN HUBBARD

Production Accountant
MIKE SMITH

Line Producer
JANE ROBERTSON

Costume Designer
PAM TAIT

Production Designer
CLAIRE KENNY

Editor
NICK MOORE

Original Music by
ADRIAN JOHNSTON

Director of Photography
JAMES WELLAND

Co-Producers
FRANK MANNION AND GEORGES BENAYOUN

Co-Executive Producers
MARINA GEFTER
GARY SMITH
CHRIS CRAIB

Executive Producers
NIK POWELL
STEPHEN WOOLLEY
DAVID M. THOMPSON

Screenplay by
COLIN BATEMAN, based on his novel

Producer
ROBERT COOPER

Director
David Caffrey

CAST IN ORDER OF APPEARANCE

Young Starkey	ADAM BLACK
Starkey's Brother	SIMON MAGILL
Dan Starkey	DAVID THEWLIS
Patricia Starkey	LAINE MEGAW
Woods	GEORGE SHANE
Margaret	LAURA FRASER

Mouse	ALAN MCKEE
Patch	'STRAPPER'
Paul, Sub Editor	BRIAN DEVLIN
Joe	SEAN CAFFREY
Taxi Driver	BRONAGH GALLAGHER
Charles Parker	RICHARD GANT
Lift Attendant	BIRDY SWEENEY
Michael Brinn	ROBERT LINDSAY
Reporter	KATIE TUMELTY
Alfie Stewart	IAN MCELHINNEY
Billy McCoubrey	BJ HOGG
Pizza Shop Boy	GERARD QUINN
Agnes Brinn	KITTY ALDRIDGE
Robert Brinn	DALE KIRKPATRICK
Voice of Robert Brinn	JONATHAN COLLIER
'FTP' Skinhead	PHILIP YOUNG
Sod	THOMAS HOURICAN
'Space Hopper' Man	DANNY KELLY
Finbar Kelly	FRANK MANNION
Giblet O'Gibber	COLIN MURPHY
Announcer	JOHN LINEHAN
Lee	RACHEL GRIFFITHS
Old Woman	BARBARA ADAIR
'Cow Pat' Keegan	JASON ISAACS
Mad Dog	PADDY ROCKS
Frankie	DEREK HALLIGAN
Waiter	PATRICK DUNCAN
Crony	DICK HOLLAND
Hood	JAMES DURAN
Balaclava	NORMAN HAGAN
Father Flynn	JOHN KEEGAN
Postal	BRENDAN MCNALLY
Civil Servant	ROBERT COOPER

Radio Newsreaders	ALISON BLACK
	ALEC FENNELL
	CHRISTINE BLEAKLEY
	STEPHEN NOLAN
	CHRIS BUCKLER

Project developed and supported by
BBC NORTHERN IRELAND

Production partly funded by
FOUNDRY FILM PARTNERS

Dialogue Coach	SANDRA BUTTERWORTH
1st Assistant Director	MARY SOAN
	KONRAD JAY
2nd Assistant Director	CLARE AWDRY
3rd Assistant Director	LIAM O'DONNELL

Production Co-Ordinator	AMY ALLEN
Assistant Accountant	LINDA BOWEN
Producer's Assistant &	
Post-Production Co-Ordinator	KATE CROFT

Locations Manager	STEPHEN KILLEN
Assistant Locations Manager	CLAIRE MCBRIDE
Locations Assistant	GARY WALKER

Art Director	TOM MCCULLAGH
Assistant Art Director	GILLIAN DEVENEY
Production Buyer	JERRY ORGAN
Art Department Assistant	CLIONA HARKIN
Storyboard Artist	KEITH HENDERSON

Script Supervisor	EMER CONROY
Focus Puller	JOHN BAILIE
Clapper Loader	ERIC GREENBERG
Key Grip	ROY HARRISON
2nd Grip	GLYN HARRISON
Steadicam Operator	ALISTAIR RAE
Script Supervisor Assistant	JEANETTE MCGRATH
Sound Recordist	MERVYN MOORE
Boom Operator	RONAN HILL
Sound Trainee	AIDEN HUGHES
Make-up Designer	LIZ BOSTON
Make-up Artist	PAMELA SMYTH
Make-up Artist	MAGGIE MAGEE
Costume Supervisor	ELEANOR APPLEBY
Costume Assistant	NUALA MCCAFFREY
Costume Daily	KERRY GOODING
Lighting Gaffer	BRIAN LIVINGSTONE
Best Boy	COLIN IRWIN
Electricians	GLEN HASTINGS
	BRENDON MCCLEAN
Special Effects Supervisor	MARTIN NEILL
Senior Special Effects Technician	MARK HOLT
Special Effects Engineer	NEIL BLACKBURN
Special Effects Technician	DONAL NEILL
	SEAN PAGEL

2nd Unit Director	NICK MOORE
2nd Unit Camera Operator	MIKE ROBINSON
	LEWIS FOSTER
2nd Unit Focus Puller	KURT SAVAGE
2nd Unit Clapper Loader	DOCHY LOWE
Camera Trainee	RAYMOND CARLIN
Clapper Loader Trainee	ANDY BRADFORD
Property Master	STEPHEN WHEELER
Standby Props	DAVE REILLY
	ALAN BRIANT
Dressing Propmen	GEOFF GEDDIS
	JIM BARR
Prop Man	VINCENT KINNAIRD
Runaround Prop Van Driver	LIAM TAYLOR
Props and Armourer Trainee	BRANDON MAWHINNEY
Armourer	ROBERT GYLE
Stunt Co-Ordinator	LEE SHEWARD
Construction Manager	RUSSELL C. FULTON
Unit Stills Photographer	MARCUS ROBINSON
Unit Publicity	VIKKI LUYA
	CORBETT & KEENE
Casting Assistants	GREG KYLE
	HILLARY HANNA
	JAMES NORRIE
Extras Casting	HILARY DONNAN

Production Runners	JEANETTE MCGRATH
	CEIRE DEERY
	JENNIE BROWNE
	BIENE POLACSEK
Post-Production Assistant	BARNABY BRAITHWAITE
BBC Northern Ireland	
Production Executives	JENNIFER MCAUFIELD
	KEVIN JACKSON
First Assistant Editor	BEN YEATES
Film Assistant	LIONEL JOHNSON
2nd Assistant Editors (Conform)	GAVIN BUCKLEY
	HERMIONE BYRT
	EMILY GRANT
	GABBY SMITH
Editing Trainee	JONATHAN HAREN
Supervising Sound Editor	ANDY KENNEDY
Assistant Sound Editor	CLAIRE SAUNDERS
Dialogue Editor	MATT GRIME
Foley Editor	JACQUES LEROIDE
ADR Editor	MIKE REDFERN
Additional Dialogue Editors	ANTHONY FAUST
	ZANE HAYWARD
Re-recording Mixers	JOHN 'BOOTS' HAYWARD
	MICHAEL A. CARTER
	ANTHONY CLEAL
Foley Artists	JASON SWANSCOTT
	DIANNE GREAVES
Post-production Supervisor	ANNIE WALLBANK
Post-production Consultant	STEPHEN LAW

Mr Thewlis' Stunt Double	JULIAN SPENCER
Ms Griffiths' Stunt Double	SARAH FRANZI
Mr Grant's Stunt Double	MORGAN JOHNSON
Stunt Performers	PAUL HEASMAN
	RICHARD HAMMATT
	SEON ROGERS
	TRACY EDDON
	STEVE STREET GRIFFIN
	DAVID CRONNERLY
	TINA MASKELL
Floor Runners	CLAIRE MULLIGAN
	CHRISTINE BRAITHWAITE
	OLIVER HOWE
	ALAN MANNING
Runners/Drivers	COLIN MCIVOR
	FREDDY BOYD
	COLIN FRIZELL
Mr Thewlis' Driver	ROBERT FLEMING
Unit Driver	PETER OGUNSALU
Unit Nurse	PAULINE MCDONALD
Dog Handler	JILL RADDINGS
	STUNT DOGS
Craftsman Joiner	WILLIAM REID
	JOSEPH DOUGLAS
Scenic Painter	ROBBIE RICHARDSON
	CHRISTIE O'SHAUGHNESSY
Standby Carpenter	ALEX ROBERTSON
	ROLAND COYNE

Standby Painter	BILLY ARMSTRONG
Standby Rigger	KEVIN KILLEEN
Stand-in for Mr Thewlis	GARY MERCER
Stand-in for Ms Griffiths	SARAH WARD
Generator Operator	CARLO MCDONALD
Electrical Tender Driver	PETE MORROW
Camera Car Driver	RAYMOND BOYD
Dining Bus Driver	ALAN GREENE
Wardrobe Bus Driver	DAVID MCDOWELL
Make-up Bus Driver	ALAN CROZIER
Security Co-Ordinator	GERRY HASSETT

FACILITIES

Camera equipment	PANAVISION UK LTD
	ICE
Lighting Equipment	FILM LIGHTING FACILITIES
Lightworks	OCULUS
Grip Equipment	LIGHTGRIP
	PANAVISION GRIPS
Cutting rooms	DE LANE LEA
Dubbed at	PINEWOOD STUDIOS
Dolby Sound Consultant	JULIAN PINN
	HOWARD BARGROFF
Film Processed at	RANK FILM LABORATORIES
Grader	JOHN HEATH
Negative Cutting by	TRU CUT
Digital Film services	CINESITE
Titles Designers	JOHN DOWNEY
	LUCY ALLEN
Titles and Opticals by	CAPITAL FX (LONDON)

Music Laid by	REEL SOUND
Location facility vehicles supplied by	G&H FILM & TELEVISION SERVICES LTD
Caterers	BRITANNIA CATERING
Costumes supplied by	CARLO MANZI
	DAMODES
Flights arranged by	THE TRAVEL COMPANY
Filters	SOUTH LONDON FILTERS
Motorhomes	CARLTON MOTOR HOMES
Radios	WAVEVEND
Stills	PINEWOOD STILLS
Translight provided by	ALAN WHITE
Legal Services	RENO ANTONIADES LEE & THOMPSON
Production Finance arranged through	BERLINER BANK A.G. (LONDON BRANCH)
World revenues collected and distributed by	MEESPIERSON MANAGEMENT AND COLLECTION B.V.
Insurance Services	AON/ALBERT G. RUBEN
Completion Guaranty provided by	INTERNATIONAL FILM GUARANTORS, INC.
Banking	COUTTS & CO.
Original score produced by	ADRIAN JOHNSTON
and mixed in 5.1 surround by	STEVE PARR AT HEAR NO EVIL
Conductor	TERRY DAVIES
Copyist	COLIN RAE
Music Contractor	ISOBEL GRIFFITHS

'BUTTERFLY LOVE'
Performed by Jim Reeves
Written by Mitchell Torok
Published by Unichappell/
Elvis Presley Music
Licensed by kind permission of
Cross Music Ltd.
Recording courtesy of BMG
Entertainment International
UIK and Ireland Limited

'BABY'S LONG GONE'
Performed by Country Punk
Written by Laurence Hardy
Published by EMI Music Publishing
Limited

'THE MAGNIFICENT SEVEN'
Composed by Elmer Bernstein
Arranged by Adrian Johnston &
Terry Davies
Published by EMI United Partnership
Limited

'THE FOUR SEASONS'
Composed by Vivaldi
Licensed by kind permission of
KPM Music Limited (MCPS)

'POLITICIAN MAN'
Written by Turlough Kelleher
Performed by Turlough Kelleher &
Wild Waters
Recording Courtesy of Scala
(Divorcing Jack) Ltd.

'KENTUCKY RAMBLER'
Composed by Richard Gilks
Published by KPM Music Ltd.

'IT'S HARD TO LOVE JUST ONE'
Performed by Jim Reeves
Written by S. Willet & F. Robison
Published by Unichappell/
Elvis Presley Music
Licensed by kind permission of
Cross Music Ltd.
Recording courtesy of
BMG Entertainment International
UK and Ireland Limited

'DREAMIN' OF YOU'
Performed by Good Luvin'
Written by Colin Beckinsale
Recording courtesy of
Scala (Divorcing Jack) Limited

'SYMPHONY NO. 3'
Composed by Dvorak
Licensed by kind permission of
KPM Music Limited (MCPS)

'THAT OLD FAMILIAR FEELING'
Written by Mike Flowers
Performed by The Nolans
Published by World International
Music Publishing
Recording courtesy of
Scala (Divorcing Jack) Ltd.

THANKS TO

Anne Aubrey
Arthur Baker
Belfast City Council
City Air Express
Emerald Isle Books
H.D. Finch's
The Europa Hotel
Eurodollar
Malone Mews
Sharon Mawhinney
Paddy McCann
McCay Cars
MMK Freight
Nick O'Hagan
1 Oxford Street Gallery
(Paul Wilson, Paul Bell)
The Royal Ulster Constabulary
Paul Staffords
VIP Taxis

WITH SPECIAL THANKS TO

Lyn Benjamin
Iain Bennett
Laurie Borg
David Bray
Mary Brehony
Malcolm Burgess
Jonathan Channon
Pilly Cowell
Phil Dale

Patrick Duncan
Mark Dunford
Gretta Finer
Michael Foster
Susan Gray
Graham Hartstone
Deirdre Hawthorne
Austin Hunter
Tim Johnson
Francesca Leahy
Pat Loughrey
Lorraine McDowell
Damian McParland
Mary Maguire
Pippa Markham
Nick Marston
Brian Mulholland
Helen Noakes
Cresta Norris
Kevin O'Shea
Dave Read
Gillian Reynolds
Steve Robbins
Tricia Ronane
Roger Sampson
Greg Schenz
Aaron Simpson
Mike Smith
Kate Triggs
Amanda Verlaque
Daniel Walker